"There's bound to be peace sooner or later," Ryne pointed out, emboldened to speak. "Commander Kurtessus said that with our weapons and the predicators and all, the primary mission of the blackjackets might be accomplished within my lifetime. If he was right, we'll be at peace some day."

The Under-sergeant shook his head. "Never, trooper. I've heard that talk before, and it's only talk. I respected Kurtessus—best combat commander I ever knew—but he did love to dream. There'll always be a mission for the blackjackets. Remember: 'Law and justice for the stars. . . .' "

The others took up the familiar words and a chorus of deep voices completed the solemn oath: " 'To this I dedicate my life and my strength, and I pledge before my comrades courage, loyalty, perseverance to the death!' "

"That's a mission that will go on as long as space exists and men cross it," the Under-sergeant said.

But Ryne knew it wasn't so.

ABOUT THE AUTHOR

John Morressy was born in Brooklyn, N.Y., in 1930. He published his first story in 1952, and has been writing ever since: novels, novellas, juvenile literature, stories, essays, fables, poetry, verse and reviews.

A Law For The Stars is his first LASER BOOK but it is the ninth book he has had published. Of these, six have been science fiction novels. He plans to write a good many more, for he finds that science fiction is a pleasure to write and it offers him the chance to work with themes that don't fit easily into works with a contemporary setting.

If there is a single theme running through all his work, he hopes it is his belief that the world would be a more pleasant place if we could accept the fact that killing one another is not an effective way of solving our problems.

JOHN MORRESSY

A LAW FOR THE STARS

Cover
Illustration by
KELLY
FREAS

Toronto • New York • London

This book is dedicated
to those who have learned,
and to those who will.

A LAW FOR THE STARS

A LASER BOOK/first published February 1976

Copyright © 1976 by John Morressy

ISBN 0-373-72021-1

Printed in U.S.A.

PART ONE

JADJEEL: THE INNOCENTS

Power, like a desolating pestilence,
Pollutes whate'er it touches; and obedience,
Bane of all genius, virtue, freedom, truth,
Makes slaves of men, and, of the human frame,
A mechanized automaton.

—Shelley

Prologue

The world called Jadjeel was settled by the last survivors of a religious sect that had suffered near-extinction at the hands of the Earthly tyrant Bordon Moran. They made planetfall only after a long voyage filled with hardship and suffering, and they had no wish to seek further for a sanctuary.

Other humanoids, the "blue folk," dwelt in the forests and among the mountains of Jadjeel, but they ignored the newcomers. The seacoast was uninhabited. The pioneers gladly settled by the water and began to build a new life.

After two generations, some of the younger colonists journeyed to farther stars. The rest remained behind to enjoy the bounty of the world they had been given.

Centuries passed in peaceful contentment. Jadjeel was a fruitful, tranquil world, and in the easy pleasure of each new day and the certainty of a good tomorrow, the past became an encumbrance. It was allowed to die. Those suffering Earthbound generations were forgotten. Their hard-won knowledge was lost. The facts of history blurred into myth and legend.

Little trace of Old Earth origins survived. Bordon Moran became a name to frighten naughty children. North America was a place as remote as the Home Beyond Death. In time, even the starfaring voyage of the first colonists came to be regarded as a symbolic tale. Surely, said these fisherfolk, farmers, and traders of Jadjeel, our ancestors could not actually have flown through the emptiness overhead. No human can do such things. It is a story passed down to teach us humility. Life began here, on Jadjeel, long ago. That is the truth; the rest is fable.

Some believed this new, reasonable view. A very few clung to the legends of their forefathers. The majority gave little thought to the question. Thus it came as a great surprise to the people of the coastal settlements to hear that visitors from the stars had been living among the forest dwellers for two years.

Ryne was a small child then, but he remembered those times clearly.

CHAPTER 1

The news arrived on a market day. Ryne's parents had laid out their goods in the customary place, by the black altarstone atop the seawall. The bargaining dish was polished brightly. The counting stones stood in neat pyramids, the gray by his father's left hand, the red by his mother's right. All was in order, all in readiness for a busy market. But no trading was done that day.

Ryne never learned who had brought the news. He only knew that suddenly everyone in the marketplace was talking, shouting, arguing. The crowd was large, and all were excited.

Many of those who heard of the visitors that day refused to believe a word of the story. The marketplace was full of merchants and traders, a sceptical lot, and they were quick to scoff. They knew how word travelled, and how much it changed as it passed from speaker to speaker, ever more remote from the event. Besides, who could know what happened in the forest? It lay beyond the plains, across the barren stretch of black rock known as Deadlands. Few went out there, and fewer came back. This "news" was all a lie, they said.

And truly, the tale was incredible. Men with green skin, black skin, mottled skin? Men with dead white skin and flame-red hair and eyes? Preposterous! the listeners said. Creatures twice as tall as the tallest among us, and others not reaching to our knees, covered with fur? Ridiculous!

They laughed at their neighbors' gullibility. Humanoids with seven fingers, or none, or tentacles where fingers ought to be? Absurd! they said, and strode off secure in their certainty that any other intelligent beings who lived in this universe were sure to have hairless bodies, be five-fingered, and of a proper size. In short, they would resemble the sensible inhabitants of coastal Jadjeel, or at most, the

9

barbarians of the forests and hills, and not some dream creatures.

But there were those who accepted the news as true, and they were much affronted. Why had such a boon befallen the savages of the forest? Why, they demanded irritably of one another, why could not these marvelous beings have come to *us* instead? We have valuable goods to trade, while the forest dwellers have only their herbs and their primitive weapons of nala wood. It was really most unfortunate, they said. And with great excitement, they proceeded to speak of an expedition across Deadlands and into the dangerous depths of the nala forest.

A few residents, when told of the news, quoted ancient sayings and hinted darkly at a time of trial near at hand. They were ignored by all.

A trading caravan was organized that very day. Ryne's parents were among the chief participants. In two days' time, a line of traders, their guards and servants, and their heavily-laden haxopods passed through the gate, crossed the plain, and disappeared into the distance. They carried with them the finest wares the coastal settlements could offer.

Ryne wanted very much to go and see the wondrous beings from the stars, but he was too little. He was left at home, in the care of his mother's threshold-sister. Once the traders had departed, he climbed to the roof of their house to watch his parents' caravan grow smaller and smaller and at last disappear. He felt very sad, and very much alone.

Ryne never saw his parents again. The entire trading expedition vanished without a trace. But about a year after their departure, an army of forest people descended on the settlements. The coastal dwellers were easy prey. They were defended—if such a term can be used—only by a flimsy palisade, for there was nothing in Deadlands to threaten them, and the forest people were only ignorant savages. But now the savages had leaders: green men, black men, red and white and mottled men, of all shapes and sizes. Some even resembled the people of the settlements.

A few offered resistance to the invaders. They were slain out of hand. The rest were spared for the service of their new masters.

Soon after the assault, Ryne's guardians disappeared. Their home and all its contents were seized by the invaders. When Ryne sought help, frightened neighbors and even threshold-kin turned him away. Alone, afraid, friendless, he huddled by the altarstone and wept. Then, wisely, he rose and dried his tears and turned his energies to staying alive.

From this time on, Ryne lived by himself. He stayed near the seawall, begging for food, stealing it when he could. He took shelter wherever it was available. It was a hard and lonely life, but for a resourceful boy, it was not an altogether unhappy one. Ryne knew a freedom and an independence enjoyed by few in the settlement. Only the presence of the conquerors made his life hateful.

Gradually the conquerors remade the coastal settlements into a chain of fortified strongholds. The flimsy palisades were replaced by walls and closely patrolled. Entrance was difficult; escape was almost impossible, and any attempt was severely punished. All new arrivals were closely questioned. If their responses were unsatisfactory, they were taken to the ruler, who called himself Overlord. Few were seen again.

Like all Jadjeelans in the settlements, Ryne endured much during these years, and everything he suffered made him hate his conquerors more bitterly. His own helplessness only deepened his hatred.

Once, while resting on the seawall, Ryne was nearly killed by one of the mottled men. They were called Quespodons, and they were very strong. For no apparent reason other than his own amusement, this Quespodon threw a large paving stone at Ryne.

If he had not been nimble, Ryne's skull would have been crushed where he lay.

Another time, two of the green creatures came upon him as he ate. When he did not greet them with sufficient respect, they threw Ryne bodily from the seawall and took turns casting fishermen's spears at him as he tried desperately to evade them. When they grew bored with the pastime, they walked off, leaving the boy to drag himself, half-drowned, from the water. No one dared to help Ryne. They feared to incriminate themselves by contact with him.

Ryne did not forget these humiliations, nor did he forget his lost family. But he could do nothing. Still not a man, still alone and friendless, he could only watch, and listen, and wait for deliverance.

The decisive moment in Ryne's young life came unexpectedly. Late one day a fishing craft tied up near the spot where he sat idly on the deserted seawall. The fisherman, who knew him by sight, asked Ryne to guard his catch while he summoned friends from shore. Ryne agreed—he would get a dinner out of this—and took his place in the boat.

The fisherman was barely out of sight when one of the small fur-covered invaders appeared on the seawall. He looked hungrily down at the shining haul of fat, delicious sotal. The little man clambered down, dropped lightly into the boat, and without a word to Ryne began to pick over the catch. The biggest, most succulent sotal he tossed to the seawall.

Ryne did not know what to do. These little men—he had heard them called Quiplids—had never done him harm, but he knew they could be dangerous. Still, he was under an obligation.

"These aren't my fish," he said. He spoke in the invaders' language, which had become the working language of the settlements. When the Quiplid did not answer, he added, "I don't know what price to ask."

"I'm not buying them, I'm taking them," the Quiplid said without turning.

"But you mustn't do that. I'm supposed to be watching—" Ryne began. The little man half-turned and struck him full in the face with his small, hard fist. Then he calmly returned to his task.

Ryne fell back, dazed, rocking the boat wildly. He spat over the side, rubbed his mouth, and rose to his feet, steadying himself with the aid of the gaff. He was hurt and angry, but it did not occur to him to strike back. But the Quiplid glanced back as Ryne arose. Seeing the boy erect, armed, blood smearing his mouth, the little man assumed an attack.

Ryne had seen what a Quiplid could do with his double-bladed knife. He had no desire to be disembowled or hamstrung. Without a thought of the consequences, wanting only to stay alive, he lunged at the Quiplid and laid open the little man's arm to the shoulder.

After that, he had no choice. The Quiplid switched the knife to his uninjured hand and drove Ryne back with quick, throat-high slashes. Ryne had seen Quiplids fighting one another, and knew what to expect. As the Quiplid ducked for the low slash that would cripple him, Ryne swung the gaff hard. It caught the little man across the skull and knocked him over the side. The Quiplid sank like a stone.

Ryne threw down the gaff in horror. He plunged into the dark water and stayed under as long as he could. Surfacing, he dove again, touching bottom, searching in vain for the Quiplid. There was no trace of him. He hung onto the boat for a time, then went under once more, but without success.

Clinging to the boat, panting and exhausted, Ryne felt a wave of awful fear. He had done the unthinkable: he had slain one of the conquerors. No one else had ever done what he had just done, though many had spoken of it. He knew what the outcome must be. He would be hunted down and eventually caught and punished in some horrible way. No one would shelter him, no one would dare to help him in any way. If he turned to anyone for help, even to his threshold-kin, they would be likely to betray him to protect themselves. His was the ultimate outlawry. His only course was flight.

He had to go at once, to give himself the maximum start before they came in pursuit. That they would pursue him and stay after him to the end, he did not doubt. But he had to try to save himself, even if there seemed to be no hope.

He had to think calmly, without giving in to panic. He must have a plan, not simply go off in aimless flight.

Ryne did not know the sea, and the time of storms was at hand. So his way lay inland, past the wall. He would cross Deadlands and go to the far mountains. It was said that tribes lived in the mountains. They might be friendly.

Ryne moved quickly. No one was in sight, and he heard no alarms; his crime had not been witnessed. Climbing to the seawall, he brought back the fish flung there by the Quiplid. With this done, he was ready to leave. Upon reflection, he decided to wait for the fisherman's return. If he went off, there might be talk about it. Others might wonder where he had gone, and why. He forced himself to wait, and even talked idly to the fisherman for a time before going off to the food stalls.

Here and there he bought bits of dried food in small amounts and tucked them into a scrip. To avoid questions, he stole a pair of water-jars and filled them after dark. There were no other preparations, and no goodbyes.

Ryne was in luck. The forest folk on guard that night were careless. He made it easily. He travelled all through the night, and by daybreak he was at the border of Deadlands.

Four days later, his food and water were gone. On the fifth day of flight, he was hopelessly lost. On the eighth day, weak and delirious, he crept into the shadow of an overhanging black rock to die.

CHAPTER 2

Ryne slept long, tortured by frightening dreams. When he awoke, his body was cold and his mouth and lips were dry. He reached out to a dark figure who sat watching, croaked a pitiful appeal for help, then fell back into his delirium.

Cool water seeped between his cracked lips, and a moist cloth passed over his forehead and closed eyes. A voice spoke close by. It was a soft, high voice, like that of a small child.

"Rest now. We will care for you," the voice said.

Fear forced a word from Ryne's baked throat. "Pursuers!"

"No one will find you here. You're safe with us. Rest."

He had been found near death by a man and a little girl who were crossing Deadlands on their way to the sea. The man was blind. His eyes were bound with a strip of cloth. The little girl was as ragged and dirty as the man. Both were of the mountain tribes. Like Ryne, they were fugitives. When he had recovered sufficiently to talk, Ryne asked them what they had done.

"This is Thone," the little girl said, respectfully nodding to the blind man. "He foretells the future."

"Is that a crime among the mountain tribes?" Ryne asked.

"I do not say what others ask to hear. I fortell the truth. That is often a crime," the blind man said in a flat voice.

"You must not go near the settlements. You won't be safe there. No one is safe since the invaders came."

"Tell us about the invaders," the girl asked.

Ryne told them everything he knew, holding back only his own reason for flight. Often one of them would interrupt him to ask for more details, or to check distances and directions, or numbers, or the placement of guards. Thanks to his hungry prowling through the settlements, Ryne knew a great deal about these things, and his answers seemed to satisfy them. He wondered why they were so curious about these matters, but he did not ask. It was not his right. Thone and the girl, Varyssa, had saved his life. In gratitude, he must help them.

He was obviously reluctant to return to the settlements, and Varyssa asked him why. Ryne hesitated and began to struggle with a confused story about finding a guide among the tribes and going in search of his parents. Suddenly Varyssa seized his wrist and placed her fingers over his lips to silence him.

Thone had moved away from them. Now he sat cross-legged in the open. His head was thrown back. The sun beat down on the sightless eyes hidden under their twist of filthy rag. His broad shoulders twitched and were still. Then he ripped the cloth from his eyes. His sinewy blue arm pointed at Ryne's heart and his blank white eyes transfixed the boy.

"Ryne will return to the settlements, and with his own hands, he will help to drive off the invaders. This I foretell," said Thone. He rocked back and forth in silence; Ryne watched with a mixture of superstitious terror and fascination. Thone's next words plucked a cry of astonishment from the boy. "You were the first to raise a hand against them, when you slew the small man in the boat. You fled, but now you must return with us. For you there is no other way."

The blind man said no more. Ryne looked to the girl, but her expression revealed nothing. He was afraid of so many things at once that he felt unable to move. These two might be mad. But the blind man knew things no one could know. Such a power could not be defied, and Ryne would not dare to try. And if they did return to the settlements, and Ryne was recognized, they would all die. It was impossible to do as Thone commanded and just as impossible to disobey.

The girl released his wrist, stood, and said, "Thone is never wrong. You will return with us."

"But we must not! If they recognize me, we'll all die!"

Thone was beside him, replacing the cloth over his eyes. He laid a hand on Ryne's shoulder and said, "No one knows that it was you who killed the small man. But if it will make you feel safer, Varyssa can change your appearance so no one will recognize you."

Ryne had no choice. He was grateful for this small protection. That night, Varyssa taught him how to stoop and twist his shoulder in a way that made him appear like a crippled old man. Once he had mastered this posture, she tore strips of cloth and tied them across his shoulders to ease the strain of the unnatural stance and at the same time make it impossible for him to stand upright in a forgetful moment. Before he slept, she had him drink a thick broth that would cause his skin color to deepen to blue for a time. Ryne did as she instructed. When he awoke, his skin was already beginning to turn the blue of his companions.

The next day, before they set out for the settlements, she rubbed a bad-smelling grease into his hair to dull its gleam and give it the ashen drabness of advanced age. When this was done, she inspected him critically and demanded his garments.

She appeared to be a girl no older than himself, but she spoke with authority. Ryne obeyed her as if she were the oldest and wisest of the altar-keepers. There was something in her ways, her assurance, her methodical approach to every situation, that made him trust her.

She took his clothes, left, and returned shortly with ragged garments. Ryne examined them with dismay.

"Where did you get these? What happened to my own clothes?" he demanded.

"Those are your clothes. I have changed their appearance, as I changed yours," Varyssa said.

"But they're older, more worn. And they're a different color. How did you do that?"

"No time to explain," she said impatiently. "Put them on. We must start."

Ryne was mystified, but he did her bidding. Varyssa had strange powers for a child.

If she was mysterious, Thone was even more so. He seemed able to foretell the future and to uncover secret acts from the past. But could he really have meant to say that Ryne would help drive off the invaders? That was impossible, surely. One boy could not drive off thirty armed men and their supporters. Thone had to be wrong. But Ryne recalled that the very reason for Thone's exile was the accuracy of his predictions.

Ryne puzzled over these things as they travelled that day. When they stopped at night, he was no nearer to a solution. If anything, thinking about the blind man and the girl had raised more questions in his mind. He had concluded that they must be sorcerers, or wizards. He was surprised to find that this did not terrify him, as it should have.

Their magic seemed beneficial. There was always a plentiful supply of food and pure water—but neither of them carried more than a small scrip and a water-jar, like Ryne's. Only sorcery could have produced a potion to change Ryne's skin, or managed to age his garments so effectively. And even their way of speaking was odd and different.

To Ryne, Thone and Varyssa spoke the language of the settlements. But they spoke it unlike the people he knew. They spoke it as if they had learned to think in another language and had to hesitate before they spoke. When they conversed with one another, they spoke rapidly in a language he had never heard. He assumed that it was the speech of the mountain tribes. And sometimes they used a third language—only quick words and phrases—that sounded like the speech of the invaders.

Whatever his misgivings about Thone and Varyssa, Ryne owed them service. That was the code of his people, and he did not think of disobeying it. And despite all the strangeness surrounding them, he trusted them. Not for a moment did he believe that he would drive off the invaders and free his people from their grip. But he knew that prophets often speak in obscure and indirect ways. Perhaps Thone meant that Ryne would somehow help persuade the invaders to treat his people less harshly, or to leave them and return to the forest. Even that would be difficult. The invaders were all-powerful and un-opposed. They would not be swayed by two children and a blind man, even if the blind man were a prophet. What could be in store, then?

He looked up at the stars that blazed overhead and wished they held an answer for him. Somehow the stars were brighter and more numerous in the skies over Deadlands. Tired as he was, Ryne lay awake for a long time, staring up at their cold beauty.

In the days that followed, Ryne plodded on over the dull black stones, his head filling with unanswered questions. At last the walls of the settlement appeared in the distance. Thone and Varyssa at once called a halt and conferred between themselves. After they had spoken for a time, Varyssa summoned Ryne to join them.

They did not answer all his questions, but they confided much in him. When Ryne led them to the gate, he was greatly reassured. He understood the prophecy and his own role in it. He was eager, very excited, and a bit fearful. But above all, he felt grateful and honored by the trust that had been placed in him.

CHAPTER 3

The trio were so ragged and woebegone that they were at first given scant attention by the guardians of the gate. But they were not long unnoticed. They had done something extraordinary: a Deadlands crossing was considered all but impossible for a small party travelling on foot. And in addition, the blind man was a prophet, led across the murderous stone waste by a child and a bent old man to seek sanctuary among the coast dwellers. This circumstance required investigation.

Before full darkness had fallen, the three newcomers were in the presence of the unsmiling green-skinned figure known to all as Overlord. In the presence of the ruler and his close attendants, they were questioned through an interpreter. Thone spoke for all.

"We hear that you come to us for sanctuary. Is this so?" the chief attendant asked.

"It is so," Thone replied.

"Why do you require sanctuary?"

"I am an exile. I foretold the future truly, and some who were displeased brought about my disgrace. I have heard that the coastal people value truth, so I had my servants bring me here."

"You crossed a deadly wasteland."

"Others have crossed it. We had no choice," said the blind man simply.

Another attendant had a question. "You come from the far mountains, and yet you speak the speech of the coast. How?"

"I speak all the tongues of Jadjeel, living and dead."

"And what do you expect from us?"

"Only the chance to live," the blind man replied.

Overlord's deep voice filled the room, silencing all others. "The coastal people no longer rule here, I do. Tell me, why should I offer shelter to a blind man, a cripple, and a child? What good are three outcasts to us?"

"I can see the future."

Overlord laughed, and the others joined in. When all were silent once more, Overlord said contemptuously, "You can see nothing. You're blind."

"I need no eyes. I have other ways of seeing."

"We need no tricksters or skillmen here. We have enough to amuse us," Overlord said.

"I know the future," Thone retorted. "If you doubt, test me."

"We will," Overlord declared. "We'll test you here, now, before you have a chance to trick us. Tell me, prophet, what do you require? Do you chew zaff leaves, or inhale smoke? Does the child sing you into a trance? We'll provide anything. You'll have a fair test."

"I require only silence."

"You'll have it." Overlord issued the command to all in the chamber. Then, to the blind man, he gave the order to begin.

The ragged prophet settled down cross-legged before Overlord's bench. Behind him knelt his old bent servant. The child knelt beside the blind man, holding his right hand tightly against her forehead. His head sank forward, lower and lower, as if he were falling asleep. One of the attendants snickered. He was rewarded with an angry scowl from Overlord. The silence deepened, and those in the chamber felt a growing sense of discomfort.

The prophet's head jerked upright as if in a spasm. His free hand tore the rag from his eyes. He pointed to Overlord and began to speak in a strong but distant voice.

"A white vessel comes to Jadjeel. . . . Bigger and broader than the oldest nala tree. . . . Many men aboard this vessel, men dressed in black, armed. . . ."

At his words, those in the chamber exchanged startled glances. Here and there a mottled hand reached for a club, a Quiplid clutched the hilt of his double-bladed fighting knife in an instinctive gesture. Overlord motioned for absolute silence and leaned forward eagerly, searching into the blank white eyes, listening for the prophet's next words.

"A battle deep in the forest. . . . Other men, not like those in black. . . . Many die. . . . On the white vessel, after, a green man at the helm, leading others. . . . Men with mottled skins, black skins are around him, and small men covered with fur. . . . Other worlds than Jadjeel become theirs, pay them homage. . . ."

"When will the white ship come?" Overlord shouted.

Thone slumped forward, limp as death. His little servant looked up at Overlord in appeal. At his signal, a pair of attendants rushed forward to lift the blind man and bring him before their ruler.

"What do you know of the blackjackets? When will they come?" Overlord demanded, struggling with the settlement speech. His green skin glistened and the air was rank with the stench of his anger. "Speak up! Our lives depend on it!"

The blind man shook off the restraining hands and steadied himself. He appeared dazed. "Someone spoke," he said weakly. "I was seized. All is gone now."

Overlord gripped his ragged robes and drew him closer. "You spoke of a white ship landing here, on Jadjeel, deep in the forest. I know those white ships, prophet. They're filled with Sternverein Security troopers—blackjackets. I thought we'd finally escaped them, but now you say they're coming here. When? Where will they land?" he demanded, shaking the helpless man.

The blind man started to speak, then collapsed in Overlord's grip. The attendants took him. The girl flung herself before Overlord and cried, "He must rest. When a prophecy is broken, he is weakened. Please, let me care for him."

"When will he be able to tell us more?"

"He must have a full day of rest, or the power becomes confused and everything is indistinct," the girl replied.

"He'll have his rest, then. I want him to be accurate when he speaks again. We grant you sanctuary, all of you," the green ruler announced for all to hear. He rose and summoned an attendant. "Put them in the secure chamber near my quarters and see that they're guarded. Have my personal mediciner inspect the prophet and do whatever is necessary. Give them anything they want. I'll have the prophet back here, and next time he'll keep talking until we find out all we need to know."

Overlord left the hall and returned to his private chambers, a suite of rooms filled with all the comforts Jadjeel could provide. He had not always lived so; but he had not always been a monarch. Even now, from time to time, he felt himself growing soft, smothering in goods and comforts, and remembered a small bare cabin with a single folding cot and weapons stowed in its curving metal walls. Overlord had abandoned space some fifteen galactic years earlier, in headlong flight from pursuing blackjackets. But a starfarer was always a starfarer. He still felt the pull of the stars in his cool yellow blood.

Posting the usual guards, Overlord dismissed his servants, extinguished the lights, and threw himself down on his soft bed to think on what lay ahead. Fifteen years of safety, and now the blackjackets were on his trail again. He cursed and slammed a hard green fist into his palm. How had they found him? No one had left Jadjeel since he and his outlaw band arrived. They had dismantled and buried their ship, the *Iraxes,* and stayed deep in the forest for nearly seven galactic years. Surely their trail had been lost. And yet the blind man spoke of a white ship and troopers clad in black. It had to be the truth. What could a blind tribesman on a backward world know of the Sternverein?

He cursed the blackjackets in his hissing native

tongue. Every outlaw in space knew that the security troopers of the Sternverein were his sworn enemies, dedicated to his extermination. Overlord had heard the tales. He had seen the troopers in action with his own eyes. It was a near miracle that he had escaped the ambush on Oxodromis. That had taught him caution and patience, and helped keep him and his band alive. But the blackjackets, it appeared, were as patient as he. And they were relentless, untiring in pursuit, and merciless in victory. It was uncanny, the way they could track down a single ship in the chartless emptiness of space, home in on one world out of thousands and lay their hands on a fugitive weary of flight. Wizardry, that's how they did it.

Overlord smiled into the darkness. Wizardry, indeed. Now he had a wizard of his own. He would be ready for the blackjackets. He stretched out, still smiling, and settled down to a night's sleep.

CHAPTER 4

Thone's two servants half-carried him to their assigned quarters. When they entered, they brought him directly to the bed, where he collapsed heavily. Varyssa listened anxiously to his breathing and turned to the chief guard.

"The prophet is very weak. He must have undisturbed rest, or he may die," she said.

"Overlord is sending his personal mediciner. If he—"

"Would Overlord have the prophet poisoned?" Varyssa broke in shrilly. "The old man and I know how to care for our master. We are the only ones who know his needs."

"But the mediciner knows—"

"Send him away. We must be undisturbed."

The guard looked unhappy, but he obeyed. He and his companion left. Only when the door had thudded shut and the bolt had slid into place did Varyssa approach the motionless figure. Anyone watching from the door would have seen her dutifully checking the blind man's vital signs, massaging his wrists and neck, and bathing his temples. But Ryne, seated opposite her, could see her lips and the blind man's moving ever so slightly. Straining hard, he could barely distinguish the faint susurration of their whispered voices. The words were beyond his perception.

He would have liked to know what they were saying, but his duty was to be watchful. He was satisfied to wait. Something was afoot, that he knew, and he trusted them to tell him all that was needful. He was ready for anything.

Varyssa at last appeared satisfied with Thone's condition. She covered him warmly, then curled up to sleep beside Ryne at the foot of their master's bed. Ryne felt her nudge him in the back and turned so he could hear her clearly. His orders were skimpy but clear. He grunted to acknowledge them, and went to sleep wondering what was to befall them.

Ryne awoke to commotion. Varyssa was hammering on the door, pleading with the guards. On the bed, Thone writhed and twisted, casting grotesque shadows in the light of the single bedside lamp. His back arched; his chest heaved; his breathing was loud and labored, erratic as the breathing of a strangling man.

"Come in quickly, quickly!" Varyssa was begging the guards. "I need strong men to hold him down. All of you, hurry, or the prophet will die!"

Ryne remembered his orders. He rose from the floor and drew back, out of the way, wringing his hands helplessly.

The door opened, and four guards entered with weapons drawn. The chief guard glanced around cautiously, then summoned the others to the blind man's bedside. He looked down on the figure now racked by exhaustion, twitching fitfully, and said, "I've brought two more men. What's wrong? What do you want us to do?"

"One of you must come over here, by me. Two at his feet. Don't touch him yet," she said.

The chief guard, a green creature of Overlord's race, gestured to the others to do her bidding. They were blue forest-dwellers, big men but slow-witted. They moved into place at his direction.

What happened next was too fast for Ryne to follow, even though he was watching carefully. Thone's feet shot out, one after the other. Ryne heard a sharp cracking noise, and one of the blue men fell heavily backward and lay still. The other clutched his throat and fell to his knees, gagging, as blood spurted from his mouth. The guard captain doubled over forward with a low grunt. Thone gripped his head and shoulder, twisted, and again Ryne heard the cracking noise. The green body slid to the floor.

Thone swung himself upright. The fourth guard lay still beside him. Varyssa was drawing a dagger from his back. Thone glanced at the body and said, "Nicely done. Let's get to work."

Ryne stepped forward. "You can see," he said, astounded. "Your eyes . . . They were blank, but now. . . ."

"An inner eyelid. It can be useful. Well, Ryne, are you ready? We have a busy night ahead."

"You killed them all," Ryne said, still bewildered.

"We executed them," Varyssa corrected him. "The invaders of Jadjeel are fugitives. They've been condemned to death by the Court of Mercy on Occuch. We are their executioners."

"Even the forest dwellers? Were they condemned?"

"They joined the invaders willingly, did their work, took their pay. They earned their fate. Don't trouble over them," Thone said. When the boy did not reply, he went on, "Think of your family and what became of them. This is your chance to pay back this space-trash for what they did to them."

Ryne did not have to think long. "I'm ready," he said.

They went directly to Overlord's chamber. His guards had been among the four dispatched, and his door stood locked but otherwise unprotected. Varyssa quickly opened it, and they entered silently. When they were in place—Ryne watching at the door, the others at Overlord's bedside—Thone awakened the outlaw leader.

Overlord started up, but winced and shrank back at the touch of a blade against his throat. In the faint light, he saw the blind prophet standing over him, looking down with the cold eyes of judgment. At the sound of a high voice, Overlord turned and saw the child standing opposite her master.

"Keda Fhelum, known on Jadjeel as Overlord, once master of the outlaw driveship *Iraxes,* you have been charged with the following crimes," she recited. "Piracy; murder; consorting with slave traders; disruption of honest trade and innocent travel. The Justiciars of the Court of Mercy have weighed your offenses and judged you guilty. The sentence is death."

Before the condemned Keda Fhelum, Overlord of Jadjeel, could scream for mercy, his throat was slit. By Thone's count, that left twenty-eight of the pirate band. Quickly and methodically, one by one, sometimes in pairs, they too were executed. Before the sun rose, justice had been done on Jadjeel.

In the morning, the coastal dwellers awoke to a strange sight. Over the gates of their fortress, mounted on the spikes of nala wood, hung the heads of Overlord and all his attendants. Not one had escaped the mysterious avenger who struck them down by night. The forest people were gone, fled to the refuge of their old home, preferring to face Deadlands rather than endure the wrath of the coastal dwellers. The settlements were free once more.

In the face of this miraculous delivery, at a time of such joy and celebration, no one gave a thought to the blind prophet and his servants. Many days passed before someone noticed that they had disappeared completely, as if by sorcery. It was a curious thing, to be sure. But it was so much overshadowed by the liberation of the settlements that it was soon forgotten.

CHAPTER 5

Before the first light broke, they were heading for Deadlands astride the fastest haxopods the invaders' stables could provide. Ryne could have returned to his old life, but he chose not to. He sensed something better in store. Thone had turned to him as they left the fortress and said simply, "Come with us, if you want to." Ryne joined them gladly.

Their destination was a cave midway between Deadlands and the foothills of the mountain range. Once inside, the barren black rock of Deadlands seemed far away. The air was cool, and a ribbon of fresh water trickled down one wall to fill a shallow pool. Ryne was surprised by the cave. He had never heard of a place like this in Deadlands. When Varyssa, with a gentle touch of her hand, pivoted a boulder at the rear wall, he was still more surprised. But when she began removing the contents of the niche thus revealed, Ryne was astonished.

"This was our forward base for the Jadjeel mission," she explained. "Our ship is hidden in the mountains. We have only the basic necessities here."

Ryne had never heard of anyone bringing a ship to the mountains, but that question vanished from his mind. He saw things he had never dreamed of. Varyssa took a rectangular white object, touched it, and one side emitted a light brighter than that of a lamp burning the purest sotal oil. It gave off no smoke, nor did it smell, and it was cool to the touch. While Ryne stared at this wonder, Thone picked up a reddish block, twisted it in his hands, and set it down. It ignited in a low, hot flame. Ryne felt a moment of doubt: perhaps they were sorcerers after all.

Thone looked at him and smiled reassuringly. "Don't be afraid. This is a fire block, and Varyssa's using a Kepler lantern. They're quite ordinary. Haven't you ever seen anything like them?"

"Never. You can make light, and fire, and you use no sotal oil," the boy replied.

Varyssa turned to him. "You'll see many surprising things, Ryne, if you stay with us."

Thone erected a metal plate over the flame and began to mix powders on it. When the powders began to liquify, he added a clear fluid and poured the solution into a cylinder. As he affixed a rounded cap, he explained to Ryne, "This will neutralize the pigmentation agent we gave you. It's faster than drinking the solution. You'll be back to your old color even before we are. Hold out your arm."

Ryne did as he was told. Thone gripped the arm firmly, held the rounded cap of the cylinder against it, and Ryne felt a momentary cool pressure. Varyssa was next, and then Thone pressed the cylinder against his own arm.

Ryne blurted out the wild thought that had occurred to him. It could not be true—but there was no other answer. "You're not mountain people. You're not from Jadjeel at all, you're from the stars, like the invaders."

"We're from the stars, Ryne, but we're not like those vermin. I'll explain things to you after we eat. You'll have the chance to make an important choice, and I want you to know what you're choosing."

Thone's words made it difficult for Ryne to keep from bolting his meal. Fortunately, the meal itself was so different from anything he had ever eaten that every morsel fascinated him. All the food came in strange hard skins. Some was hot, some cold. It was not very tasty, but it was interesting all the same. When he bit into one of the skins, Varyssa advised him to avoid them. "They're simply packaging, Ryne —protective coverings. They aren't meant to be eaten," she explained.

"But we always eat the skins."

"Those are not skins. We're eating field rations. These were made up and packed many light-years from here."

"Is that far away?" Ryne asked.

They exchanged a smile, and Varyssa said, "Yes. Very far."

Ryne ate more carefully, observing the others and doing as they did. When they had finished, Thone rose and beckoned to Ryne. "Come outside. I want you to look at the sky," he said.

Jadjeel was a moonless world with a day more than twice as long as that of Old Earth. At the midpoint of the night, the sky was a black backdrop for a brilliant blaze of starshine, uncountable thousands of points of light in every direction, with one dense thicket of stars, a twisting serpentine band of splendor coiling diagonally across the heavens. Thone and Varyssa looked up. Ryne followed their solemn gaze, watching in silence with them.

"Do you know what's out there, Ryne?" Thone asked.

"Some people say that we came from another Jadjeel somewhere out there. A place called Old Earth. But there are many more who say that's only a story."

"What do *you* say?" Varyssa pressed him.

He hesitated, then replied, "If the invaders came from out there, and you came from out there, then maybe we did, too. But I don't know how."

"If you had a chance to go out to the stars yourself, would you go? You don't have to answer me now. Let us tell you more, and think about it," Thone said. He and Varyssa sat on the bare black ground side by side. Ryne hunkered down facing them and waited. Varyssa spoke first.

"Jadjeel is not the only inhabited world, Ryne. The stars teem with life. We know of scores of intelligent races. There may be hundreds, even thousands."

"What do they look like, Varyssa?"

"Some of them look like me. I'm a Malellan. And some are Agyari, like Thone."

"Half Agyari, half Old Earth," he corrected.

"Aren't any of them ugly, like the invaders?" Ryne asked.

"*Ugly* is a meaningless word. They're different, that's all. You don't think we're ugly, do you?" Varyssa asked.

"No, not at all."

"And yet we represent three different races. Some of the other races are very tall, some very short. Their skins are of many colors. You've noticed that among the invaders. Even among my own people, there are considerable differences. Some of us stay as small as children all our lives, and others grow to be Thone's size, or even bigger."

"Then you aren't a little girl?"

She laughed brightly. "I'm afraid not, Ryne."

"Different races have different physical features, too. The Threskillia have a pair of tentacles at each shoulder. Very handy they can be, too. And one branch of the Agyari, my people, still transmit the nictitating membrane—the inner eyelid. You've seen how useful that can be," Thone said.

"Can all Agyari foretell the future?"

"No one can foretell the future, Ryne. I told those vermin what I knew would terrify them, that's all."

"But you read my mind! No one knew about the Quiplid."

Thone shook his head. "You told us all that yourself. You were delirious when we found you. You talked quite freely."

Ryne pondered this revelation for a moment, then smiled at them. "You fooled me, but I'm glad you did. Tell me more about the other people out there."

"The important thing is that in one respect they're all the same. They all want to possess their own world in peace," Thone said. "True, they often fight among themselves for reasons that are not clear to other-worlders, but all races in the galaxy want to know that their homeworld is safe from slave traders and marauding bands of outlaws. Every space traveller wants to know that he can cross the stars in safety.

Every merchant wants to be able to send his goods to other worlds without fear of piracy. These desires unite all intelligent beings, however different they may be in other ways. They all realize that without laws and people dedicated to enforcing those laws, civilization is impossible."

"I understand. We have laws in the settlement, to regulate marriage and building of homes," Ryne said.

"And does everyone obey these laws?"

Ryne was shocked by such a question. "They must! There is no other way."

"Did the invaders obey them?" Thone persisted.

The concept of threshold-kinship was hard to explain to anyone from outside, but Ryne tried. "The invaders were . . . they were not *of us*. They were unaware."

"So they defied the laws."

"Yes," Ryne admitted.

"There are other unaware creatures roaming the stars, Ryne. Far too many of them. They land on a remote planet—a planet like Jadjeel—and commit every crime against humanity that their minds can devise. They attack helpless traders and transports in space, steal the goods and carry the crew and passengers off to sell as slaves. They believe that the galaxy is too big to govern, too big to police, and they're confident no one will ever bring them to account," Thone said, with anger growing in his voice.

"But they're wrong," Varyssa broke in gently.

"Yes. This lot found that out. Fifteen years on the *GSC,* they hid on Jadjeel, and there was no sign of them all that time. They thought they'd escaped—Overlord said so. I wasn't even as old as you when they dropped from sight," Thone said, nodding to Ryne. "But we found them and punished them, and the galaxy is that much better for it."

"Is this what you do? Just the two of you against all the unaware creatures among the stars?" Ryne asked, awed by such an undertaking.

"We're not alone. We belong to an organization created to bring law to the stars. We pursue all who threaten the welfare and freedom of the civilized races. However long it takes, we hunt them down, and when we find them, we punish them, just as we punished the invaders of Jadjeel," Varyssa said.

"Our organization is the Sternverein. It began as a peaceful league of traders and merchants. But you can't trade if your ships and goods are stolen and your crews are killed, so the Sternverein formed a security branch to protect the members and punish those who attack them."

"Why did you come to free Jadjeel?"

Thone answered, "We came to execute sentence on the crew of the outlaw driveship *Iraxes*. That involved freeing the settlements as well. A sort of bonus."

"How did you know they were here? How did you find them? If the galaxy is so big, how could. . . ."

Varyssa laughed softly at the barrage of questions, and Thone raised his hands to silence the boy. "We can't give away our secrets, Ryne, but there's a way of finding out. We have to return to Occuch to report on our mission. They'll probably send a follow-up force here to provide protection in future, and the sooner we can arrange that, the better for your people. And since we must return, Ryne, how would you like to come with us and train for the Sternverein Security forces?"

"Me?"

"I think you'd be a good trooper. The earlier you start, the better prepared you'll be. You're strong and smart, and you have courage. You know how to wait and when to act, and you can follow orders."

"You don't panic under pressure. You have better judgment than some people much older than you," Varyssa added. "These are qualities that make a good trooper."

"You think about it, Ryne, and think carefully. If you want to go back to the settlement, we'll take you there. Your threshold-kin won't turn you away now. You'll be a hero. And we'll see to it that you're well rewarded. You'll have everything you need for a comfortable life," Thone said.

"That would be nice," Ryne said wistfully. "I've never really had anything since my parents went into Deadlands."

"There's a lot to be said for a safe, comfortable planetary life. You could settle down here, and probably become an important leader of the settlement one day. Of course, you'd never see what's out there," Varyssa said, looking up to the stars.

"No, I wouldn't," Ryne said.

"Blackjacket training is pretty tough, anyway. Not everyone comes through. I think *you* would, Ryne, and I'd be proud to recommend you. But it would be a much easier life if you just stayed on Jadjeel."

"Safer, too," Varyssa added.

"Oh, yes. Much safer. You'd probably survive to be an old old man, Ryne." Thone paused, sighed, and then went on, "But if you'd like to use your life to make the galaxy a better place . . . well, think on it. Tell us in the morning."

In the morning, the three of them left for the driveship in the mountains. Ryne never saw Jadjeel again.

CHAPTER 6

The journey was long even at lightspeed, but Ryne did not find it boring. The exhilaration of newness precluded not only boredom but also fear and doubt about his future. He felt only anticipation.

He began to learn the common language of space at once. At first he used the speaking box with the tiny knob that fit inside his ear and recited lists of words for him to repeat and memorize. As his vocabulary grew, he worked with his hosts. His fluency increased rapidly. Soon all their conversation was in the common tongue, and Ryne found himself thinking in it as easily as in the speech of Jadjeel.

With this tool, he learned even faster. Each day brought him something never dreamed of on Jadjeel. He struggled to master a variety of new skills. Intricate machinery soon became as familiar and as manageable as the counting stones of his abandoned world. He lived in a state of constant excitement. With tasks to perform and a full program of exercise and study, he was busy from the moment he awoke until he collapsed on his narrow bunk.

After one strenuous exercise period, Thone announced that these sessions were to be shortened in the future. Ryne was to undertake a new activity. It was a very important one and would fill much of his time until planetfall.

"If you're going to be a trooper, you have to know about the Sternverein and its history," Thone told him. "We have all the information on board. I want you to learn everything you can before we reach Occuch."

"Will you teach me?"

"We're not teachers. Varyssa will show you how to operate the information center. It's easy enough."

"Why don't you and Varyssa tell me about the Sternverein instead?"

"We have machines that do it better than we can. Besides, we have other duties."

Ryne sensed the futility of complaining. He would have preferred learning from his friends, but he was long accustomed to making the best of unsatisfactory situations. In any event, here was something new. It sounded promising.

When Varyssa showed him the cubicle that functioned as the ship's information center, though, his heart sank. It was smaller than some of the cramped alcoves he had slept in on Jadjeel. She seemed to read his unspoken thought.

"It looks small, Ryne, but you'll find that it's just the proper size for what it has to do." She slipped into place at the console, adjusted seat and headpiece, and quickly ran down the controls. Satisfied, she gave place to Ryne.

The console was simple to operate. It had only two banks of controls, one for the sound tapes, the other for the visual prisms. Once their positions were memorized, they could be worked without removing one's eyes from the viewscreen. Ryne moved the seat to a comfortable position, brought the headpiece down to rest on his shoulders, and looked at the blank gray rectangle ahead. He was ready.

"You learn quickly," Varyssa said. "That's good. The more you know when we reach base, the faster you'll move ahead. I'm going to insert the full historical cycle from exodus to founding and mission. I want you to learn it in detail."

"I will, Varyssa."

"You may not grasp everything at first. This isn't a trainer, it's a reinforcer-refresher for field units. We'll help you if we can."

"Will I learn about Jadjeel?"

"Forget Jadjeel. That part of your life is over." Varyssa held up a tape-disc in one hand, a prism in the other, and displayed them before she locked them in place, saying, "What's on here is what concerns you now. Ready?"

"I'm ready," Ryne said coolly.

But the sudden apparition brought a cry of surprise from the boy's throat. He was unready for such a sight as this. Before him hung a blue and white ball, turning silently against a backdrop of stars. It was Earth, where the age of starfaring had begun, and it was breathtakingly beautiful. Ryne felt himself drawing closer and closer to that tranquil sphere. As his vision penetrated the cloud cover and approached the surface, a gentle voice came to him through the headpiece, like a friend speaking close behind him.

The voice spoke of the old days, the grim days, the days before exodus. The images began to change. For a long time, Ryne saw no more beauty.

Earth in the twenty-first century had been a monstrous place. Drought and famine and outbursts of plague struck ever more frequently and ferociously. Death tolls were sometimes counted in the millions. Xenophobic wars erupted without warning, raged for a day or two, then ended abruptly. The participants, having exhausted all their resources, withdrew into glowing ruins to die dreaming of revenge. The great power blocs were incapable of action. Human society became a cockpit of warring tribes. All law was forgotten in the frenzied scrabble for food and water, air, and living space.

Then came Wroblewski, the Emancipator, the last great mind of Old Earth. His calculations were never fully understood, but his instructions could be followed. He gave mankind the drivecoil, and the drivecoil gave them the stars.

The first Wroblewski driveship rose from a launching ring in a land called Siberia in the year 2083 A.D. of the Old Earth/Galactic Standard Calendar. Thus began the exodus.

The desperate populace of Old Earth fled like fugitives to the stars. They sent out no probes to learn what might await them. It no longer mattered. Whatever was out there could be no worse than what they had made of Old Earth. All they asked was escape. They were not running to a better life, they were running from a terrible one. They cooperated in one last effort to survive. When the last of the driveships lifted from its ring in 2192 A.D. it left the rotting, denuded husk of a planet whose children for more than a century had devoted all their resources and all their energies to escape.

Fewer than four of every ten pioneers touched down again alive and unimpaired in body and mind. For them, the long crossing was a horror to be blotted from memory forever. If another humanoid race dwelt on their new planet, the children of Earth offered friendship. If necessary, they gave battle. But they would go no farther. Human roots were implanted in alien soil, and the first wave of the exodus ended.

But on every new world, the driveships towered to mock the settlers. Those ships, the last great product of Earth technology, were created to span galaxies, not to stand idle after a single voyage. While the first generation of pioneers shunned them in terror, their children and grandchildren looked on them with eager eyes. They could not long resist the challenge to press on. They were a new breed, born to starflight, and for them the ships held only promise. Thus the second wave of the exodus began, spreading the seed of Earth in an ever-widening sphere. For no one turned back. All went outward, to the unknown and the unexplored.

In the centuries that followed, Old Earth and its history were forgotten. Records were scanty; books were scarce; memories were dim. The wisdom and experience of millennia were fragmented and scattered across a thousand worlds, or lost forever. Only human nature remained.

In the early days, the great enemy was the unknown. As the second wave of exodus continued, man reasserted his position as mankind's greatest threat.

Piracy was reborn. For centuries it had been conducted by well-dressed men with high-sounding titles. Now it resumed its ancient form. In the reaches of space there were no treaties, no contracts, no agreements—no law. There was only force.

Unlike their originals, who lived in times when piracy was often the only way for a free man to survive, these new pirates were pirates by choice. The galaxies offered habitable worlds and the chance to amass great wealth honestly. They chose to be worldless and live off the suffering of others. They struck without warning, took what they wanted, and withdrew at their leisure into the trackless void, confident that none could pursue. Other races, following the lead of the Old Earth descendents, produced their own pirates.

Piracy was not the only new plague. Planets were badly underpopulated, machines were scarce, work was hard and often dangerous, and the work force was small. The market was ripe for slavery. The Daltrescans, semi-civilized inhabitants of Altresc, learned of this institution of Old Earth. By a variety of methods, they acquired a fleet of driveships and soon became the slave traders of the galaxy.

Those who had fled farthest from the barbarities of Old Earth became the easiest targets for the new barbarities of space. There seemed to be no refuge in the galaxy from the inhumanity of humans toward one another. It appeared that the sorry history of Old Earth was to be re-enacted, unchanged, on a galactic scale.

Then came Leddendorf, the Lawbringer.

He was the first great figure of the interstellar age. His family were among the early free traders who had helped to weave a tenuous network of trade routes to join the emerging worlds. It became an article of faith to Leddendorf that without freedom to travel and trade in safety, the new stellar civilization could never be more than a scattering of isolated outposts, each one in constant danger. Progress would come to an end.

Leddendorf created the Sternverein. And to guard the white ships of his trading fleet, he summoned brave and dedicated men and women from all the worlds to form the Sternverein Security Troops. From the moment of its inception, the force grew in numbers and skill. Soon the pirates and slave traders learned to fear the white ships and blackjacket troopers, and to flee at the very sight of them. But the troopers pursued.

Thanks to Leddendorf, law was coming to the stars. Much had been accomplished, but much remained. The goal was unchanged: free trade and free travel for free worlds.

Ryne listened, fascinated. He was learning the history of space. It was a partisan view of history, the carefully-worked Sternverein version, and so it did not tell everything. It was sometimes inaccurate, sometimes wildly distorted. But Ryne could not judge that. He believed. To doubt the evidence of the tapes and prisms never occurred to him. This was revelation, and the very fact that he was on a drive-ship, in the company of starfarers—a starfarer himself—made it undeniable. He was utterly convinced, ready to believe all he was told and question nothing.

To a boy whose race had lost its past, this was an awesome experience. The universe burst upon his mind, reverberated within him, changed him forever.

Ryne thought no more of Jadjeel, of parents and threshold-kin, of his own early days. All that was over. After this, he thought only of his future as a Sternverein Security trooper. He had found his mission. He would dedicate his life to bringing law to the stars.

CHAPTER 7

The first day on Occuch was one of the busiest and most confusing in Ryne's life. This was the center of Sternverein operations, a world of contrasts that dazzled the newcomer's mind.

Wonder succeeded wonder. They landed on a rocky plateau in the center of a wilderness. Minutes later, they were walking in a cave of metal. A strip of bright light ran overhead. Thone called the place a *tunnel* and said there were many more on Occuch. Men and women dressed in black were also in the tunnel. Some were on foot, some riding in silent wheeled vehicles unlike anything Ryne had ever seen. No one spoke to anyone else. Ryne had many questions to ask, but since Thone and Varyssa seemed disinclined to talk, he kept silent.

They boarded one of the vehicles, and it moved off at a speed Ryne found uncomfortably fast. When he saw that the others were relaxed, he calmed down. The tunnel dipped downward at a slight angle, then levelled off. Soon they emerged into a clearing with an enormous white cube in the center. Here the vehicle stopped.

The white cube was the largest structure Ryne had ever seen. Using doors located all around the base, people were entering and leaving it every minute. The three entered, and Thone spoke briefly to a man behind a glass wall. Almost immediately, another man came out from behind the glass and looked closely at Ryne.

"We have to report now," Varyssa said. "Seadhal will take you to your quarters and see to your testing. We'll visit you when we can."

"Do your best, Ryne. We've recommended you for blackjacket training, because we think you've got the makings of a trooper. You'll have to prove it to others, now," Thone said.

"I'll prove it."

"Follow me," Seadhal said, and started off at a fast pace.

Ryne hurried along behind, trying to duplicate the big man's smooth fast walk, but failing. His legs were too short. Out of breath, half-running, he kept his thoughts off his discomfort by studying his guide. He was something like Overlord, but Seadhal was not green. His skin was a gleaming blue-black. His skin and uniform blended into one dark mass, flashing points of silver on collar and shoulders, and that made him seem even bigger than he was.

They re-entered the tunnel, but soon turned down a narrower branch, through a door, and into a small room that moved rapidly upward. Again Ryne felt a momentary panic, and again he fought it down. He did not want to appear fearful before this man.

At the top, they entered into a wooded area on the planet's surface. Ryne looked behind them at his first opportunity, but he could see no trace of the little room, only thick trees all around. Seadhal led him to a group of low dunelike shapes that rose in a clearing. He pushed open a door Ryne had not even noticed. They went into a room furnished with one bunk, one locker, and one chair.

"Here you stay. Clean yourself," Seadhal said.

In an adjacent room, a steady stream of water trickled from a tube overhead and went down a hole below. Ryne stripped and washed.

When he came out, his old outfit was gone. In its place lay a folded coverall, boots, and a cap. He put them on and went to the other room, where Seadhal waited.

The black man inspected him critically, then said, "First we eat. Then begin the tests. Come."

They went into the clearing again, and entered a larger building. A few people were in this one. Some were dressed in black, like Seadhal, but most were in coveralls. Some of them glanced curiously at Ryne, but no one spoke to him.

Seadhal was silent throughout the rather tasteless meal. When he led Ryne back to quarters, he paused and said, "Soon they come for testing. If all tests you pass, training begins on the ninth day."

The question of what happened should he fail the tests came to Ryne, but he held it back. It was well that he did, for it would have counted against him. His testing already had begun on Jadjeel, when he agreed to join Varyssa and Thone. To Seadhal, he said confidently, "I'll see you in nine days, then."

Seadhal left, and a woman soon came to take Ryne to one of the low buildings. He spent many hours here. People placed flat plates against his chest and back. They listened to his internal functioning, sampled his bodily fluids and even his breath, and shone lights into his eyes and ears and down his throat. They asked him questions and gave him tasks to perform. Some of the tests were easy, some impossible, some ridiculous. One person would be kind and friendly to him, and the next would be brutal. Sometimes the same person acted both ways in turn.

Ryne took it all, good and bad, and did exactly as he was told—no more and no less. These people did strange things, but he assumed that they had reasons he did not yet understand. They fed him, and he had a good place to stay. He trusted them.

On the morning of the ninth day, he was awakened early by a heavy fist hammering on the door. "Now you eat. Then begins training," a familiar voice said.

Ryne had passed all tests. His new life began that morning. Because of his youth, he was placed in a pre-training course. Even so, the early years were difficult for him. The Sternverein Security force made little allowance for age. Young or old could be of service, if they were good enough to qualify.

Now all the hard lessons of Ryne's boyhood came to his support. He had known hunger and fatigue. He had suffered exposure to heat and cold, lived for days in wet clothing, forced himself to work through fevered bouts of sickness. He could do it all again, for a greater goal than mere survival. Others older and stronger than he dropped from training one by one. Ryne endured.

By the time he reached the customary recruit's age, Ryne was already one of the best in his group. He never stopped working to improve himself. He mastered three forms of unarmed combat. He became expert with every weapon in the troopers' arsenal. He proved that he could survive in any terrain, elude any pursuer, track down any quarry. He obeyed an order precisely, quickly, without question. Obedience became a reflex. Ryne was the perfect trooper.

His old freedom, the freedom of the outsider and the loner, was gone. He lived now by a rigid time-table established and enforced by others. But he considered this—when he thought of it at all—to be a gain rather than a loss. He was no longer alone. He was part of something important and good. He belonged.

The training went on for four years, and then Ryne was ready. The final ceremony was held at night, on a high plateau. The fledgling troopers were received into the Sternverein as the stars hung in blazing welcome overhead. Awards and honors were distributed, and several of them went to Ryne. As the climax of the ceremony, a crescendo of voices repeated the great oath: "Law and justice for the stars! To this I dedicate my life and my strength, and I pledge before my comrades courage, loyalty, perseverance to the death!" Ryne felt a pride and happiness such as he had never before known.

Many tales were told that night, and toasts were drunk to the memory of those who had gone before. But amid the reverent talk of the heroic dead, one white-haired old veteran inserted a cold cautionary note. He was Colonel Zoss, sole survivor of the driveship *Huntsman's* clash with a pirate crew. Zoss had lost an arm in that battle on a nameless world of unending rain.

"I'd like to go out again, with a crew like this bunch," he said. "We'd clean up space for good."

"How do we compare with the crew of the *Huntsman?*" someone asked him.

"You're better. Oh, they were a fine bunch in combat, don't mistake me. But you're better trained. Your equipment is better. In those days, the scum we hunted had all the experience. They were smarter at the game. We didn't have predicators then. We hunted, and guessed, and hoped, and trusted to our luck to track them down. It's amazing we caught up with as many as we did." Zoss shook his head, laughed softly as if at himself, and said, "If we hadn't had a man like Blesser, and that castaway skillman to trick them with his voices, we might not have caught up with that last lot. As it was, we paid dearly."

"But you did the job. You were all heroes."

"Maybe we were all fools," Zoss said. A few angry mutterings came from the darkness—hero or not, Zoss was pushing his privileges hard. He laughed again, that soft mocking laugh, and said, "Fools to die, not to fight. Don't you do as we did, or they'll call you fools, too. Survive, troopers. You're valuable. The fact that you've made it this far sets you apart. You're stronger and smarter and braver than the rest of the galaxy. We gave you tools for performance and survival in a dangerous job. Performance *and survival,* troopers. We did *not* train you to be heroes and saviors and die gloriously in a noble cause. We trained you to execute justice on condemned spacetrash—to disinfect the spaceways, and survive to do the job again and again until it's over and done with. We have all the heroes we need. It's live troopers who get the work done."

Others had unkind words to say about Zoss, but Ryne agreed with him. It was all very well to die bravely, but quite another thing to die needlessly.

And perhaps many of the old heroes had done just that. He thought this, but kept it to himself. He did not want to argue. This was a night to be enjoyed.

The next day was less pleasant. Ryne reported in the morning for his first regulation Nolo treatment.

The process was painless but lengthy. Ryne was put into a condition of semi-stasis that lasted for three days. His mind remained receptive to external stimuli, and he was given a full final briefing by means of training tapes. But his body was anesthetized. Basic physiochemical alterations were being induced of which he remained completely ignorant. He knew only that they were necessary to the mission, and their effects would not harm him in any way.

Nevertheless, the effects of Nolo were always the subject of some apprehension among first-timers. Tales told by their instructors and old space hands did little to put them at ease. Their concern was understandable. The troopers were young and healthy, and Nolo was a sexual suppressant. Although none were aware of it, a similar substance had been mixed in their food during the entire training cycle, but its effects were temporary. Space duty required Nolo. Once the treatment was completed, the effects of Nolo were permanent until chemically reversed.

The reversal treatment was unpleasant, but totally effective. All the younger troopers submitted to it willingly, and were completely restored within sixty hours. Old starfarers, though, tended to take fewer and fewer Nolo scrubs, as they called the reversal treatment. This was not entirely due to the discomfort involved.

In time, Nolo had a damping effect on all emotions. Sternverein Security troopers felt not only an absence of sexual drives, but also a steady diminution of their capacity for strong feelings of any kind. Their long training left them conditioned to act on reflex, and their decisions were made solely on the basis of logic. When aggressive drives were needed,

they could be triggered by the use of stimulators—
blue pills taken before combat contact.

Nolo had one serious drawback. It inhibited
normal production of a digestive enzyme. This lack
could be offset by additives in the ship's rations, but
without the additives, a trooper on Nolo soon suffered acute indigestion and disabling stomach cramps.
Troopers were therefore conditioned to depend on
ship's rations for survival, and to look upon all
planetary food as poison.

· Survival on alien foodstuffs—provided they were
not otherwise toxic—was possible, but it was at best
a difficult and uncomfortable process. The Sternverein considered it wisest to forbid the eating of
planetary food, and to severely punish any disobe-
dience of this rule. Each trooper on space duty was
required to carry twelve days' supplementary food
concentrate at all times. Since the troopers never left
their wounded behind, and since no prisoners were
taken on either side in their battles, a twelve days'
supply was deemed more than adequate.

Troopers complained about Nolo occasionally,
but did as they were ordered. Whatever its draw-
backs, Nolo was essential to the effective operation
of the Sternverein. It assured discipline on long
space runs, and enabled mixed crews to work in close
quarters without emotional stress that might jeopar-
dize success of the mission. It avoided sexual com-
plications in alien contact situations. It enabled
troopers to enter combat situations thinking not of
home and family, but of their duty. Nolo was useful
to the organization; therefore, the individual trooper
had no choice but to accept it.

Ryne underwent the treatment without a hitch. At
first, he noticed nothing except that his rations tasted
better than they ever had before. He was unaware
that the change was not in the food, but in him.

On the day after the Nolo process was completed,
Ryne boarded the driveship *Blesser* on Nemesis Run
K622. It was a pursuit mission.

PART TWO

SPACE: THE LAWBRINGERS

CHAPTER 8

Ryne settled easily into the routine of space duty. Driveship life was much like a continuation of training—a sequence of watches, exercise sessions, weapons' practice, study, and rest, in regular progession. He did not mind. This was the life he had worked for, and he found it good.

He was the youngest trooper aboard the *Blesser*, and the reputation won on the training grounds of Occuch had preceded him. These facts made him the fair butt of all the taunts that veterans have heaped on recruits since men first bore arms together. Ryne kept his peace and bore it all. He knew that when the time came he would prove himself, and the taunts would end with his acceptance. Even now, his performance in the weapons area had silenced all but Over-sergeant Gothrun, and he was a Skeggjatt. His people looked upon speech as a medium for boasting. When they were not using it thus, they were quite taciturn.

Whatever his role among the seasoned veterans, Ryne was soon undisputed chief of the compartment he shared with the other newcomers. At first reluctant to defer to an equal in rank, they soon unbent to acknowledge his skill in the tools of their profession.

Ryne found his shipboard companions much like the men he had known in training. Like him, many were alone. The parents of some had been slain by marauders, while others had lost their families to slavers, or to the plagues that still struck from time to time to decimate scanty planetary populations. Now they had only the Sternverein. It was family, home, church, nation, and friends to them.

Recognition soon came to Ryne from other quarters. When he left the ship's information center after a session with the prisms on tactics, he was summoned to the commander's cabin.

Commander Kurtessus returned his crisp salute, then seated himself and indicated a seat for Ryne. "You're off duty now, trooper. I've gone over your records and I want to talk to you. Unbrace. Pour yourself a mug of scoof," he said amicably.

Ryne went to the steaming cylinder. "One for yourself, Sir?"

"Yes, thank you. That batch has been simmering for three watches. It should be good and rich."

Ryne filled two mugs with the hot black liquid. A pungent aroma rose on wisps of steam and scented the bland air of the compartment. They sipped cautiously at the scalding brew, and then Kurtessus set his mug down and asked, "How far have you come on the tactical program, Ryne?"

"I completed C21 today, Sir."

Kurtessus furrowed his broad brow and searched his memory. "That's a tough one, as I recall. Let me see. . . . Forest terrain, second encounter, numerical and weapon superiority to the enemy . . . three attack options."

"That's right, Sir. Good memory."

"I won't forget that last one soon. Never did manage to solve it properly. I expected that problem to keep me back from promotion. You're coming along fast, Ryne," Kurtessus said.

"Thank you, Sir. I enjoy the tactical problems."

"I see that you worked under Trainer Seadhal. He must have put you through every problem on the prisms ten times over."

"He did, Sir. He was a good trainer."

"The best on Occuch." Kurtessus took another sip of the bracing scoof and said, "You did well in your studies, too. Tell me frankly, Ryne, how did you like the program in Cultural Groupings? You got good ranking, but were you really interested?"

"Yes, Sir, I was. That's a valuable program. Slaver crews are homogeneous, but on any given pirate craft there might be a mixture of as many as ten unrelated races. The collective psychodynamic, if we can key into it, can be a powerful weapon for us, especially . . ."

Kurtessus raised a hand good-naturedly to silence him. "You sound like a predicator, Ryne. No need to give me the whole program. The reason I asked is that we have an advanced CG program in the ship's information center. I want to assign it to a man who's interested in it, because I've found that a man always works better on a subject that interests him. Would you like to train for an Alien Cultures specialty?"

"I would, Sir. The better we understand them, the more effectively we can fight them."

"True enough, Ryne." The commander rose, drained his mug, and set it down. Ryne remained respectfully silent, sensing that there was more to come and awaiting it with growing interest. Kurtessus was turning out to be different from his expectations of a blackjacket commander, and Ryne wondered what other surprises might await him.

After a long pause Kurtessus went on, "It may not always be that way, though. We'll run out of enemies one day, and then there'll be other work to do. If we're not ready, all this could be wasted effort . . . wasted lives."

"What other work would a trooper do, Sir?"

Kurtessus rubbed his blunt nose and drew his brows together in concentration. "How old are you?" he asked.

"GSC, Sir?"

"No, no, no," the commander said impatiently. "GSC is for the historians. I mean bio-subjective. Your physical age, Ryne."

"Eighteen, Sir, as near as I know."

"Eighteen. And you've completed the Sternverein standard field medical program?"

"Yes, Sir, I have."

"In that case, Ryne, you at eighteen know more

CHAPTER 9

Shipboard predicators had guided the *Blesser* to a single-star four-planet system and designated the innermost planet as the probable site of the pirate base. Their accuracy was one hundred percent. Three watches following Ryne's talk with his commander, the alert signal sounded.

The *Blesser* had emerged from drivespeed into sublight at a height roughly twice the maximum range of planetary scanning equipment. The ship's scanner-override detected and neutralized six warning devices, and the *Blesser* then proceeded to make a full series of survey runs. With all data gathered, the ship touched down in a perfect manual landing in a clearing ringed by heavy forest. Two hundred kilometers away lay the pirate camp.

Guards were posted to the *Blesser* and the base camp. Ryne was not among those picked. He went with the assault force. He gathered his equipment: standard battle kit, rations, pistol, knife, and shortsword, as always. For this operation he also took hand scanner and override, climbing gear, and oxygen, as well as extra rations. With all in order, he submitted to Gothrun's inspection, then assembled with the others for the commander's briefing.

In full battle dress, his long-barreled pistol slung across his chest, Kurtessus looked far different from the relaxed senior officer Ryne had spoken to so recently. His voice was clear and toneless as he recited findings and orders.

"This is a low-oxygen planet, gravity .936 Occuch standard. Rotation period six days GSC. Approximately one hundred and four hours of light remain, and the mission must be completed before dark. We will operate on chronometer time. Oxygen is to be used as needed. No human or humanoid life forms extant; one major predator. Closest planetary an-

57

alogues are Trintal I, Oba Minor, and Kess," the commander began. "Tactical situation C17 on approach, changing to B9 immediately upon visual contact."

Ryne went over the tactical prisms in his memory, calling the training patterns before him. C17: heavy forest, enemy strength uncertain; B9: bare upland, enemy in view, positions strong. Weapons superiority uncertain; advantage of surprise to assault force.

Kurtessus went on to give details. "The encampment is on the upper level of a stepped plateau. Directly below is a group of rectangular objects, origin and purpose unknown, no evidence of current use. We will strike the encampment at precisely eighty-eight hours. Synchronize at zero . . . now. Provisional assault plan Seven."

Ryne found that Kurtessus had picked the very plan he would have chosen for this situation. Seven was a three-stage attack that turned the momentum of the enemy's natural reactions into a weapon against him. It was a good plan when numbers were uncertain, and ideal for this terrain. Under Plan Seven, the assault force divided into three unequal groups. The smallest struck first, in a noisy frontal wave, to drive the surprised enemy back. There, in the rear, the second, larger force, awaited them. When the enemy recoiled from this second blow, the first group fell aside to permit their headlong retreat into an ambush formed by the third and largest group.

Ryne hoped that he would be in the first or second group, and have a chance of direct contact. The third group was really nothing more than a firing squad, mopping up the broken remnants of a defeated enemy. But then Kurtessus spoke again. "We have located the enemy ship. It is a third-stage cruiser and appears to be in excellent condition——a desirable prize, not to be destroyed. Over-sergeant Gothrun will take two troopers: mission, to seize and guard the ship. The rest will form as follows:

first assault group will be led by Under-Lieutenant Eohric, second by——"

Gothrun's heavy hand fell on Ryne's shoulder. The Over-sergeant summoned him with a nod of his head, and Ryne felt a twinge of disappointment. Nothing more, thanks to Nolo. He would not be a part of the assault force. He was going off to stand guard over a captured driveship, kilometers distant from the scene of action. The others would have their battle stories to tell after this engagement, but he would not. No chance to prove himself this time, unless . . . no, even if the driveship were under guard, there would be no more than one or two sleepy men to be dispatched. But it was for the good of the mission, and he did as ordered. He walked after Gothrun, ignoring Trooper Herril, who fell in behind him. No one spoke until the Over-sergeant called a halt out of hearing of the others.

"We start now. We have less distance to cover, but it's a harder way. The enemy ship must be secured by the time of the attack. I'll give you the full assault plan when we stop to rest. Any questions?" Neither trooper responded, and Gothrun said, "Then we move."

He was a husky man, but he slipped like a shadow through the thick lowland jungle growth. Ryne and Herril kept close behind, maintaining his fast pace. By the end of the first long march, they had covered sixty-two kilometers. Elapsed time was 18:14 hours.

When Gothrun mentioned the distance, Ryne said, "That's good travelling, isn't it? We'll be there ahead of schedule."

"This was the easy part," Gothrun responded. "We have to cross a gorge, and then we have a range of hills. It's low, but the rocks are crumbling, dangerous. We stop here. Security measures one-four."

It was a stringent security level, and the first indication that this might be a hazardous detail after all. Security at the one-four level called for a perimeter of wide-angle short-range scanners, plus one man on full alert at all times. It seemed an excessive caution to Ryne, but before he could speak, Herril voiced his question.

"Will they patrol this far from base, Sarge?"

"No. Security is against the predators. If one of them stumbles on us we have to kill it quietly. No firing."

"What are the predators like?" Ryne asked.

"Quadruped, carnivorous, height range 1.5 to 1.8 meters when erect. Chief weapons are foreclaws and a dewclaw just below the elbow joint. Vital spots directly between shoulder blades, front or back; below rib cage on either side."

"Knife?" Herril asked.

"Shortsword. You have to penetrate muscle. Thrust, don't hack. They're thick-skinned." When no question came, Gothrun went on, "Now we make camp. Regulation four-by-four. Herril, you decontaminate. Ryne, help me set the scanners. We'll go over the attack plan as we eat. Let's not waste time."

The first rest period passed without incident, and they started through the forest at a fast pace. Something paralleled their path for a time. They heard it clearly, but could not see it. It fell behind as they emerged into thinner upland growth.

They came to a grassy ledge that gave way to naked stone and than ended abruptly. Ryne, on his belly, looked over the sharp edge at a slender strip of muddy water that crawled below. He dislodged a chip of rock and watched it bound off an outcropping and vanish into the deep shadows.

Gothrun issued a warning.

"Don't slip, Ryne. It's three hundred meters to the riverbed."

"How are we crossing, Sarge?"

"Ropes. Didn't they teach you that on Occuch?"

"They did. But they told us to look for an easier way first."

"The nearest crossing-place is a thousand meters

from here. Get the gear ready, Ryne. You're first across."

They were at a point where the gorge narrowed to a little less than twenty meters. Near the opposite bank was a cluster of squat, cage-like trees with multiple trunks entangled under a canopy of tiny shimmering leaves. They were much like the peandi trees common on Oba Minor. Gothrun, the biggest of the three troopers, hurled the grapnel, making firm contact in a tree with his first toss. Ryne fastened his end of the rope as high as he could, for a fast smooth slide to the opposite bank. Gothrun inspected the fastenings and sent him off.

It was an easy crossing. Ryne dropped to his feet just short of the gnarled trunk-tangle of the tree in which the grapnel had lodged. He had checked his oxygen fitting, inspected the purchase of the grapnel, and turned to signal the next man across when a sudden crashing came from the bank behind him. Three predators burst from the low growth on his left and stopped in a half-circle facing him. Ryne drew his shortsword and knife and set his back against the cage-like thicket of peandi trunks as four more of the creatures appeared. The three nearest started toward him. They made no sound.

Ryne knew he could handle this as long as he kept his head. The odds were bad, but the situation was not desperate. Help was on the way. The tightly woven tree trunks protected him from attack in the rear, and he stood on higher ground than the predators. One sustained burst of his pistol and the encounter would have been over. But the order was no firing; the mission came first. It would be blades only.

The shortsword was a deadly close combat weapon, razor-sharp along both edges and finely pointed. Even so, it was no more than a fair match for the natural equipment of the predators. They were moving in now, still silent, and Ryne studied them closely, observing every detail.

The shaggy hair on their heads and torsos gave a deceptive impression of mass; actually, they were smaller than Ryne had expected. The biggest one barely reached his chest, standing upright. Their heads were broad and flat, heavy-jawed, wide of nostril, thrusting forward on thick necks. The chests were huge, encasing lungs of a size sufficient for this thin atmosphere. Their forearms were long, bristling with claws. They held them high, elbows raised and forepaws close against the chest, claws outthrust, shielding the vital spot. Ryne noticed that they moved their forepaws freely upward and outward, but were less easily able to strike downward. His higher position, then, was more to their advantage than to his. He would have to wait for them to strike up at him, then drop under their guard and hit from below. He brandished the knife, holding the shortsword tight against his thigh, and waited.

The first one closed. Ryne raised his knife as if to strike down; the creature's claws flew up; Ryne brought up the shortsword and felt it drive through muscle and grate against bone. Nearly gagging on the carrion stench of the creature's last breath, he put his foot into the predator's belly and thrust it back, against another of the pack.

In the momentary confusion, Ryne struck again, dropping to one knee and thrusting the shortsword up under the second predator's ribcage. He drew back into the shelter of the trunks, ready, waiting. Five remained, and they hesitated to press the attack. He heard a creak of branches from the peandi tree and the sound of booted feet landing heavily behind him.

"You've got help, Ryne," came Gothrun's voice.

Sword in one hand, knife in the other, the big Skeggjatt came around the trunk-tangle at a lope, heading straight for the knot of predators. Ryne joined him, snarling a challenge. The creatures broke and fell back, frightened, dropping to all fours and bounding confusedly from side to side. They began to bark wildly. Three more fell before Herril joined his comrades and the two surviving predators fled headlong.

Gothrun cleaned his blade on a broad leaf. "You kept your head, Ryne. Good work," he said.

"Thanks, Sarge," Ryne said. It was the first praise he had received from Gothrun, and it was sweet to his ears.

"Let's get these carcasses over the edge. Maybe the others will be too busy looking for their friends to chase after us," Gothrun told them. "We'll stop to rest and eat when we reach the hills."

The air was cooler and thinner when they left the forest behind them and reached the grassy uplands that rose to the foot of a low range. They increased their oxygen flow here. They saw no further sign of the predators, no trace of other life except for the small hopping creatures that fled before them through the heavy grass. They ate, rested briefly, and moved on to the cliffs.

The range burst out of the ground as if it had been forced upward at one stroke by some forgotten cataclysm. This, and the gorge, were a puzzling contrast to the peaceful grasslands, just as the timid hopping creatures around them were so different from the forest predators. This nameless planet was the only one Ryne had ever seen apart from Jadjeel and Occuch. He had heard of strange worlds, and now he was walking on one. He found the reality even stranger than the promise, but the Nolo effect kept his curiosity and excitement to a minimum.

The sheer wall of streaked and crumbling stone before them was unlike anything in Ryne's experience. He had climbed every mountain on Occuch, but none were like this. It looked difficult and dangerous. But the enemy ship lay beyond it, and it had to be climbed.

Herril readied his equipment. He shielded his eyes,

looked up, and tugged experimentally at a jutting rock. It broke off in his hand. "This is bad stuff to climb," he said. It was not a complaint; merely an appraisal.

"It doesn't get any better. This is the lowest point, so we picked it for the ascent," Gothrun said.

"Why don't these cliffs wash away?" Ryne asked. "There must be rain on this planet, and one good storm ought to bring them down. They can't take much erosion."

"Then maybe there isn't any rain."

Ryne couldn't help but protest.

"That forest requires a lot of rain, and there's a river in the gorge. The water has to come from somewhere."

"Save the planetary studies for later, trooper. The cliffs are here and we have to climb them. Get going, Herril."

It was clear why Gothrun had picked Herril for this detail. He was long-limbed, slender, and very strong. He had the reach to grope for the unseen hold just at fingertip's end, and the strength to pull himself up by the smallest grip. Watching him pick his way up the perpendicular face, Ryne knew he was seeing a first-rate mountaineer.

But this was no ordinary climb. Herril was about ten meters over their heads when a fall of stone drove Ryne and Gothrun back from the cliff base. Herril moved laterally, and before he had gone arm's length, the spot he had left split and crumbled. He worked over to a solid vein and resumed the ascent. A few meters higher up, the rock began to fall away again. Herril swung quickly to his left, kicking his toes hard into the rock face. It crumbled away as fast as he could gouge a hold. One foot broke free, then the other. He dangled by his hands for a moment, scrabbling for a foothold. The cliffside was falling to pieces under his grip. Then a great chunk gave way and Herril was carried down in a cloud of rock and dirt and choking dust, landing heavily at the foot of the cliff.

Ryne reached him first. He was unconscious, injured, but alive. Ryne was already cutting away Herril's sleeve when Gothrun joined him.

"His knee is hurt, and he's broken his left forearm. Might have hurt his ribs, too," Ryne reported.

"I'll take care of him. You start climbing."

Ryne had to speak now. "Sarge, for the sake of the mission. . . ."

"What about the mission?" Gothrun challenged him. "Don't try to take command, Ryne. Follow orders."

Ryne had no wish to do otherwise, but logic compelled him to press the point. "We've lost one man, Sarge. If the same thing happens to me, you'll be alone, and you'll still have to get up this cliff."

"I know that. So?"

"There has to be a place nearby where the rock has crumbled enough to make an easy climb. Let me look for it, Sarge."

Gothrun considered it for a moment, then nodded. "Go ahead. I can give you forty minutes."

Ryne checked his chronometer. Elapsed time was 39:44. Fewer than fifty hours remained to strike time, and they were short one man, with the cliff still before them.

He set out at a trot over the smooth ground, looking for the rockslide he was sure would be there, and as he proceeded, he thought about the mission. So far he had learned much, and more was sure to come. For the first time, Ryne grasped the difference between training—even the best and most demanding training—and the real experience of battle. Plans had to be made, but the finest plans could fall apart before one's eyes. There were more variables, more random factors, than could ever be taught or foreseen.

Ryne pondered that, and checked himself abruptly.

One thing was certain: the blackjacket trooper. He could depend on his own strength and skill, and that of his comrades. Whatever unexpected force they might have to face—men, or beasts, or nature, or even something beyond all those—they could face it and overcome. It was weak and foolish to doubt that they would succeed in this mission and all that followed. They were doing a good and a necessary job. They *had* to succeed, if the people of the galaxy were ever to live in peace and security. To brood about possible failure was disloyal.

Even as the thought occurred to Ryne, he caught sight of what he was seeking. A rockslide had bitten deep into the cliff. The softer rock had been crushed and had filtered to the bottom of the debris. Shafts of firm stone, leaning inward, formed a ramp to the top. The angle of incline was steep, but a man could walk up without the aid of climbing gear. He tested it out, and raced back to Gothrun.

The Over-sergeant had splinted Herril's arm and leg and moved him to a niche in the cliff. Ryne sat beside them.

"I found a place, Sarge. Two kilometers in that direction. We can walk up," he reported.

Herril opened his eyes, focused on Ryne, and muttered indistinct words. He shut his eyes again and drew a deep breath. Ryne looked anxiously at Gothrun.

"The kneecap is smashed, but the arm isn't bad. It's the ribs that bother him," said the Over-sergeant.

"What will we do about him?"

"Move him as far back in here as we can, and set up an automatic defense. Six decontaminators, triggered by scanner."

"Will that be enough?"

"You saw the chests on those predators. They're deep breathers. One lungful of full-strength decontaminator will finish the biggest of them."

They quickly readied Herril's defenses. He revived again, and was able to understand them, though he said very little. Gothrun explained the arrangement, and Herril nodded.

"Remember this, Herril: no firing before eighty-eight hours, or you might give away the assault. No matter what happens, don't use your pistol before then," Gothrun said.

Herril's reply was barely audible. "Understand. Mission comes first."

"You'll be all right," Ryne assured him. "There's probably nothing bigger than the hoppers this far into the uplands. We'll be back for you, Herril."

The injured trooper shut his eyes and nodded. Gothrun laid a hand on Ryne's shoulder, and they withdrew. They had done all they could for Herril, and time was passing.

They reached the top at 41:16 hours. Before them extended an empty plain. Patches of tough grass clung to bare stone, outcroppings of striated yellow rock thrust at sharp angles to the sky, and a steady cold wind pressed against them.

Gothrun pointed to the horizon. A strip of dark green ran across it. "There's more forest ahead. We'll stop there."

They moved quickly over the stony ground and reached the downward slope of grasslands at 43:51. A forest lay directly ahead. It was quite unlike the one they had traversed earlier. The trees were oddly shaped: very tall, but no thicker than Ryne's wrist. They were bare to the very top, and then they burst into a canopy of soft fronds that lifted and swung with every breeze, spangling the forest floor with an ever-changing mantle of shadow. It was a pleasant place, and they rested here for two hours, alternating guard, before moving on. The second long march ended at precisely 52:00 hours. The pirate driveship lay thirty kilometers ahead of them. The next march would end at their objective.

Ryne ate with a good appetite and slept soundly. He had taken a stim immediately upon landing, and the primary effects were upon him. He was eager for the encounter.

CHAPTER 10

They first saw the driveship at 79:08 hours. It stood in a valley, poised for lift-off. They were two kilometers away, but even at that distance, through far-scan glasses, the ship was a thing of heart-catching grace and majesty. The silver form glowed dazzlingly bright under a sun still near its midday zenith. From each outer drivepod a smooth curve drew the eye upward to the spired prow that pointed to space.

"What a prize!" Ryne whispered.

"A third-stage cruiser. One of the finest in space. It's bigger than the *Blesser,* and half again as fast." Gothrun studied the ship and its surroundings carefully, and passed his far-scan glasses to Ryne. "Look underneath."

Ryne studied the base of the ship. There was a landing ring supporting the drivepods and base.

"No record of a ring here. It must have been built secretly and kept off the charts. This planet is a more important place than we thought," Gothrun said.

"The ship's heavily guarded, too. I counted four, and there may be others in that building."

Gothrun extended his hand, and Ryne returned the far-scan. The Over-sergeant studied the square guard shack for a time, then lowered the glasses. "Six, all armed. There are two by the building. They're careless, though. Look at them, clustered together like that."

"And we haven't run into a single scanner yet."

"We could work our way in, and then one good burst. . . ." Gothrun fell silent then. Ryne looked at him curiously, and the Over-sergeant said, "I'm thinking out loud. No firing, I know."

"It'll be hard taking them any other way, if they stay so close together."

"It will. That's odd, too. It's not like this kind of

spacetrash to guard a ship so closely." Gothrun shook his head, perplexed, and said, "Come on, let's move in. Take two stims right now. Keep the override at maximum range and have your knife ready. We're close enough to start meeting people."

A kilometer from the ship, they located and neutralized the first scanner. Moving more slowly, they found three more before they stopped at a suitable spot, a cluster of broken boulders on the inner slope of the valley wall. From here they had a clear view of the ship and the guards' shelter. It was a perfect field of fire, but neither of them mentioned that.

Gothrun studied the situation in silence. Below them, the driveship's guards were loosely clustered outside the low square shack. A Quespodon was seated with his back against the wall, his short stocky legs extended, fast asleep. A Skeggjatt sat on a bench beside the doorway, cleaning a rifle. Nearby, two more Skeggjatts and two Thorumbians were noisily involved in a game of nakk. Four firearms of varied design stood against the shack wall, near the sleeping Quespodon. A single burst from their pistols would have taken the lot. Gothrun frowned, but showed no further sign of frustration.

"How far to the base?" Ryne whispered.

"Less than a kilometer. It's no good. They'd hear firing."

They were at an impasse. Two men armed only with blades do not attack six and hope to overcome; not even when the two are blackjackets. There was too much open ground to cross, and no chance for surprise. If even one guard escaped, if a single shot were fired, they had failed and placed the entire mission in jeopardy. So they waited, and watched.

Ryne conceived and discarded one attack plan after another. They could work around the building, dispatch the nearest two and seize the weapons . . . and one of the others might escape to warn his comrades. So that was useless. Create some diversion, attract two of the guards to investigate, and return in their clothing . . . and that would only work if the Skeggjatts came to them. Neither Ryne nor Gothrun could pass for a Quespodon or a Thorumbian.

There was nothing to do but wait. Ryne checked his chronometer. It was less than three hours from strike time.

Gothrun noticed him doing this. He whispered, "We'll wait. That's all we can do now. If we get a chance, we'll take them. If not, we'll open fire at strike time."

Ryne nodded. It was the only workable plan for these circumstances, but still not satisfactory. The traditional practice on a raid like this was to close off the escape routes before attacking. Cutting things too closely meant risking escapees, and escapees were doubly dangerous. They knew what to expect next time.

Gothrun and Ryne took alternate watches for the next hour. Then their hand was forced. Two of the nakk players exploded in loud argument over cheating. There was a scuffle, and a Thorumbian was sent rolling in the dust. He arose shouting, and threatened one of the Skeggjatts. The Skeggjatt drew his knife, and the others stood back to watch the duel.

Gothrun nudged Ryne. "If they get excited, there may be shooting. We have to get to those guns first."

"What if they rush us?"

"They won't if we have the weapons. Let's go."

They moved through the low brush as quickly as possible to a point behind the windowless guard shack, then worked around to the edge of their cover. Here they faced the blank side wall. The front wall, where the weapons rested, was to their right. Farther to the right, about equidistant from the building, were the two disputants and their audience.

Ryne tensed for the dash. As he awaited Gothrun's word, the Skeggjatt by the doorway laid aside his rifle and started to walk toward the duelists. By now, that affair had dwindled to a contest of invective amid a cloud of settling dust and much bold talk.

"Perfect!" Gothrun whispered. "I'll cover the five. You get the rifles and cover the Quespodon. Careful of the doorway. There may be someone still inside."

It went very smoothly. In a few moments, the six guards were squatting in the dirt before the shack under Ryne's pistol. Gothrun had checked the building and stored the weapons, and was now busy inside.

"You're a new one, aren't you?" said one of the Thorumbians.

"Sure, he is. Look at the nice new uniform," said the other.

"I bet you'd like to pull that trigger. Wouldn't you like to blast us down, kid? Then everyone would think you're a man," the first one said, and laughed.

Ryne did not reply. Gothrun stepped to the doorway. "Ignore this space trash. Their chief tells them we kill all prisoners. That's how he gets them to fight, I guess."

"How do they get an old man like you to fight?"

"Yeah, what do they promise you?"

Gothrun walked over to the Thorumbians. "Shut up," he said.

One of them did so immediately. The other said, "Too bad, old man. If you can't kill us, then you'll just have to listen to us."

Gothrun kicked out fast and caught the Thorumbian flush on the side of the skull. He sprawled back and lay still. A thin trickle of blood ran down his blue-black temple and dripped into the dust.

"Now I don't have to listen to you," Gothrun said. He looked at the others. No one challenged him.

For something more than an hour Ryne and Gothrun sat facing the six. The Thorumbian came to after a time, but said nothing further, merely moaned and held his head.

At last Gothrun cleared his throat loudly. When he had Ryne's attention, the Over-sergeant glanced meaningfully at his chronometer. Ryne understood. It was 87:57 hours.

"On your feet, all of you," Gothrun ordered.

"We're taking you back to our base. Get moving."

"Blackjackets don't take prisoners," said one Skeggjatt.

"We don't need all of you. One is enough, if you get troublesome. It's up to you."

Slowly, suspiciously, the prisoners rose to their feet.

"You're going to be tied before we go. Turn around and spread, arm's length apart. Keep your hands behind you," Gothrun said.

When their backs were turned, he levelled his pistol and waited. The rattle of distant firing came across the mountains, muted by its passage but unmistakable to their waiting ears. Gothrun squeezed off a shot. Before his second shot, Ryne had opened fire. The pirates were flung forward by the impact of the bullets, hurled face-down in the dust as if by a blow from a giant hand. One of the Skeggjatts struggled to his knees and turned to face them, his eyes wide in astonishment. Ryne sent him sprawling with a second shot, and he lay still.

It was all so different from what he had anticipated: very quick, very easy, almost automatic. It was totally impersonal. In no time at all, simply by squeezing a trigger, moving one finger less than a centimeter, six lives were ended. Ryne felt a mild surprise, but was otherwise numb. No hatred, no sorrow, no satisfaction, no pity. Nothing at all. Gothrun's voice seemed to come from far away.

"Cover me. I'm going to make sure they're finished."

The Sternverein pistol fired a soft-nosed thumbsized slug. The six were indeed finished. Ryne and Gothrun dragged the carcasses into the guard shack. Ryne took up a position in the shadows just inside the doorway. He had a clear view of the approach from the main camp. Gothrun, behind him, studied the weapons they had taken. He said little, but his grunts and low mutterings made it clear that the Over-sergeant had found something impressive. Finished with his inventory, Gothrun seated himself beside Ryne, back to the wall.

"This is a well-equipped bunch. Best ship I've ever seen outside a Sternverein base, and now these weapons. Two of the rifles are Rugatcz V long-range models. You can't get better than that," Gothrun said.

"What about the rest?"

"The usual junk. They'll fire anything, and then jam on the second shot. These Rugatcz rifles, though . . . if they have this kind of equipment at their main camp, our assault groups are in for some hard fighting."

While I shoot down prisoners, and guard the doorway of a dirty hut, Ryne thought. He did not feel that he had contributed anything to the mission so far. He was trained for combat, not merely extermination. He wanted the chance to prove himself.

It came quickly. Before him, on the brow of the hill, two running figures loomed and then vanished into the bush. Another quickly followed, then two more, and then too many to count.

"They're coming, Sarge. At least twenty."

Gothrun dropped beside him and looked out. "They must have broken through the second attack group. Quick, pop two more stims. We have to hold them until the others get here."

Ryne gulped the blue pills and asked, "Can we board the ship and fight from there?"

"Too late for that. They'd be on us before we got the ramp down, and then the ship would be theirs," Gothrun said. He slid away from Ryne, and returned almost at once with the two Rugatcz rifles, fully loaded. "Use one of these until they get close."

Ryne laid his pistol aside and fitted the slim, slightly off-center stock of the rifle into his shoulder. It was a comfortable weapon. He took careful aim at a big Skeggjatt, leader of a group of four pirates crashing through the brush about a hundred and fifty meters straight ahead. He squeezed the trigger, and the rifle eased back ever so slightly. The Skegg-jatt was flung violently up and back. Ryne picked off two of his companions before the fourth one disappeared into cover. He managed to get one more before the first return fire.

"How many did you get?" Gothrun asked.

"Four."

"I got five, I think. That cuts them by nearly half."

"Where did they all go?"

"They're trying to figure out what happened. They'll be coming at us soon. They don't have much time, if they want. . . ."

Four figures moved up fast, crouching low. Both troopers fired, and both missed. Others began closing on the guard shack. Three went down, but the rest reached the edge of the clearing.

"They'll try to pin us down. Get away from the door. Keep the ship covered," Gothrun ordered, edging aside.

Ryne rolled parallel to the front wall, covering the driveship through the narrow angle of the open doorway. For a moment all was still. Then a volley poured into the entry, chipping the heavy stone doorposts and lintel. Scattered shots followed, then a second volley, and then the first of the pirates burst through the opening, a pistol in either hand, firing wildly. Gothrun's shot caught him in the chest and flung him back against the one behind him, but then the rest came on in full force. Ryne emptied his pistol into them, and still they came. But by now the stims, adrenalin-activated, had released their full potency, and Ryne was a wild man. He slashed with his shortsword, clubbed with his pistol barrel, drove his fist and foot into bodies and faces close enough to touch, and still they fought. Ryne's oxygen tube was ripped loose. He fought on, panting for breath. The little hut seemed packed with slashing weapons, the stink of sweat and blood and smoke, the roar of confined firing and the screams and oaths of the injured and battle-maddened. And then a last burst of fire came, the familiar fire of Sternverein pistols, and it was all over.

They had to lift two bodies off Ryne, but he was able to walk out of the hut unaided. Once outside, he felt a sudden dizziness, and staggered back against the pockmarked wall, now deep in shadow, and cool. Someone pressed an oxygen tube into his face. He inhaled deeply, and his head cleared. He raised a hand to his brow, and was surprised to have it come away with blood. My blood? he wondered. He looked down and saw the long rip in his arm, and he knew. His fingertips were icy and his throat dry from the effects of stim. There was a pain in his side, as well. Then someone was talking to him. An Under-lieutenant. Ryne saw the insignia, but could not raise his eyes to the face.

"Good work, trooper. You held them here."

Ryne grunted a reply. Two troopers carried Over-sergeant Gothrun from the shack. There was a gaping red cavity in his chest, and his face was gone.

"Gothrun's dead," Ryne said. His voice was hoarse, and sounded strange to him.

"He took his share with him. The mission's a success. You'll be cited for this action, trooper."

"Herril. He was injured. We had to leave him."

"We'll send a party back for him. You need medical aid, trooper. This way," the Under-lieutenant said.

Ryne took two steps after him, and remembered nothing more until he awoke aboard the *Blesser*.

CHAPTER 11

Ryne's first mission was a success. The entire pirate crew was executed, their ship and a good supply of weapons seized, and a potentially dangerous base was claimed for the Sternverein. But it was a costly victory. Kurtessus, Gothrun, and five troopers were killed, and three others badly injured, in the assault. Herril had developed pneumonia, and was close to death when the recovery party found him; he passed the long voyage in stasis.

Ryne's own injuries were not so serious. He was fully recovered and ready for his next assignment when the *Blesser* made planetfall on Occuch.

Once Ryne was able to leave the lazaret and mingle with the others, he found the inbound trip a great improvement. He was one of the troopers beyond doubt now, a blooded veteran with a tale of his own to match any of theirs. They had heard of the battle in the guard hut, and wanted the details. Ryne gave these with precision and then leaned back, at ease among his peers, to hear their stories of past encounters. It was here that he learned how their commander had died.

The others seemed reluctant to speak of it at first. Finally, an Under-sergeant said, "He got careless. Maybe I shouldn't say it, but. . . ."

"Then don't say it," someone cut in.

"I was right behind him. I saw the whole thing. Commander Kurtessus did something no recruit would do. He dropped his guard, just for an instant, and that was all it took."

"How did it happen? Where?" Ryne asked.

"When they broke through the second assault group, all of us in the third moved up for support and pursuit. We were going through their camp when a kid crawled out of one of their huts," the Under-sergeant began.

"Sure it wasn't a Quiplid, or a Malellan?" his antagonist asked.

"It was a kid. Kurtessus stopped for a second. I don't know what he was going to do, but he didn't have a chance to do anything. There was a Skeggjatt in the hut. He nearly took the commander's head off. I got him and the kid, but Kurtessus was dead. Died instantly."

Ryne thought back to his talk with the commander. If only Kurtessus had followed his own advice and killed without mercy, he would be alive now. What had made a tough old veteran hesitate in the middle of an engagement? He had told Ryne to kill them all, women and children included; and yet he had hesitated at the sight of a child and been killed. A man like Kurtessus would not have forgotten his stims. There was something troubling in this, something Ryne did not understand and did not wish to think on.

"It's too bad. He was a good man," Ryne said.

"He wasn't Old Earth. That's what made him hesitate. Deep down, he didn't have the killer instinct," said another trooper. He nodded approvingly to Ryne. "You've got the Old Earth blood in you, that's certain."

"My people always said we came from Old Earth. There were some on Jadjeel who didn't believe it, but I did," Ryne said, with more enthusiasm than fidelity to truth.

"Old Earth blood makes the best blackjackets."

Another trooper, of Thorumbian descent, took issue with that statement. "I've seen Quiplids with killer instinct. Some of my own people have it. We're not Old Earth."

"I didn't say it was exclusive to Old Earthers," said the first speaker. "They just have it stronger than the rest."

"Mostly Old Earthers on the First Expedition. They did some mighty impressive fighting, I hear," someone said.

"Got a lot of people killed in the process, too," observed the Thorumbian.

"It was war. People die."

"Did all those refugees on Pendleton's Base have to die? I heard that the Expedition command blew up the whole planet, just. . . ."

"I never heard about that," the first speaker broke in. "Somebody's been lying to you. There were no atrocities and no war crimes. The Expedition was out there fighting to save the humans and humanoids of this galaxy, and a lot of people were sitting back snug and safe, light-centuries from the blood and the dying, telling lies about their defenders. And before the century was out, they had gone behind the back of the Third Expedition and made peace with the Rinn. Peace," he repeated, spitting out the word like a curse.

"There's bound to be peace sooner or later," Ryne pointed out, emboldened to speak. "Commander Kurtessus said that with our weapons and the predicators and all, the primary mission of the blackjackets might be accomplished within my lifetime. If he was right, we'll be at peace some day."

The Under-sergeant shook his head. "Never, trooper. I've heard that talk before, and it's only talk. I respected Kurtessus—best combat commander I ever knew—but he did love to dream about the day when there'd be no more piracy, no more slavery, nothing but peace among the stars. It's a nice dream, but no more than a dream. There'll always be a mission for the blackjackets. Remember: 'Law and justice for the stars. . . .'"

The others took up the familiar words, and a chorus of deep voices completed the solemn oath: "'To this I dedicate my life and my strength, and I pledge before my comrades courage, loyalty, perseverance to the death!'"

"That's a mission that will go on as long as space exists and men cross it," the Under-sergeant said.

The argument ended. Ryne returned to his compartment more certain than ever that it was a fine and noble thing to be a part of the Sternverein. And not an unimportant part. He was no clerk, no recorder, translator, loader, merchant, counter—that swarm of buyers and sellers who needed other men's protection to survive their daily rounds. He was a security trooper, a protector and lawbringer. He looked around the small compartment, holding his gaze in silent respect on the two bunks that were folded back, empty for the inbound voyage. Troopers Malgo and Banact had died on their first mission. But they, too, were a part of the brotherhood, like Kurtessus and Gothrun. They had pledged their lives, and fulfilled the pledge—as he too might be called upon to do one day. Ryne never forgot that.

He went to sleep with proud words ringing in his memory: courage, loyalty, perseverance to the death . . . law and justice for the stars . . . my life and my strength . . . to the death. . . .

FOR his actions on his first nemesis run, Ryne was awarded the Combat Star. On his second run, the *Blesser* went to Diundran, a watery world where triple moons sent wild tides crashing on the naked rock of some fourscore land masses and the few inhabitants lived on floating islands of vegetation. Legends told of rafts the size of cities on that world, the homes of a golden-scaled people who travelled in fish-drawn seasleds and tended lush undersea gardens.

But the legends lied. There was no beauty on Diundran. No towered cities floated on the bright waters, no golden men and women gleamed in sea and spray. There were only mud-colored, half-aquatic humanoids who guided their tangles of rank weed through the safe channels that wove among the flotsam of the racked world. There was that, and there was death.

The troopers' work on Diundran was simple, and their mission was quickly completed. The outlaw band they pursued had all succumbed to the Gathan sickness. Their flesh was slowly liquefying, while their vital organs swelled to grotesque size until they burst the skin. Most of the fugitives lay dead and rotting on the floating weed-clot no native would approach. The rest were in their terminal agonies. Execution was an act of mercy.

RYNE's third nemesis run was very nearly his last.

At first, all went smoothly. The predicators directed the *Blesser* to Hingwoll III, a planet similar in some ways to Occuch. It was slightly larger, with a gravity of 1.02 standard, and slightly colder, but these factors seemed unimportant. The gravitational increase was negligible, and the *Blesser* carried full cold-climate gear.

The pirate driveship *Yuyav* was located on the fringe of the polar region. There was no trace of human habitation nearby, yet Hingwoll III was known to be inhabited. The natives were little more than savages. Nomadic hunters, they lived at a subsistence level and produced nothing of value to Sternverein traders. There was no contact with them.

The *Blesser* scanned the equatorial belt, then the temperate zones, and found nothing. Only the scan of the polar region showed a number of small settlements actively occupied. The hunt would begin here.

Commander Brocmal had the ship put down about twelve kilometers from the pirate craft. Scouts went ahead, and returned to report that the *Yuyav* had sustained damage in planetfall. It was tilted sharply to one side, and the hull was pierced. Without repairs impossible to make on this planet, it would never lift off again.

Brocmal placed a three-man guard on the *Blesser*. With the rest, he set out for the nearest Hingwoldin village, three days' trek into the polar region.

The air of Hingwoll was breathable without special equipment, and the troopers were grateful for this. The cold-climate suits were bulky, and each man carried sixteen days' food concentrate in addition to his normal combat gear. As they moved deeper into the polar regions, the air grew colder, but remained pure. Walking became more difficult in the forest, where they encountered new-fallen snow. Urged on by Brocmal, they made good progress in spite of the hard going, and arrived at the village late on the third day of travel.

The village was deserted. A pervading musky smell indicated recent occupation, but no one was to be found. A drying frame with a few flintlike strips of meat still stood by one of the high conical huts, and some leather bottles of a bad-smelling liquid were found in another, but nothing more. Brocmal set the men to a close search, and they found the sign they sought. In one shelter were footprints unmistakably left by a spacer's boot. At least one of the fugitives lived.

A heavy snow had begun to fall and the short day was ending. There was no point in trying to follow now. The troopers spent the night in the village and set out early the next day, under clear skies. Brocmal led them to the neighboring village, still hoping to get information from the natives.

They passed through a dense wood, crossed a frozen lake, and at a narrow pass beyond it, with snow falling once more, they met their first Hingwoldin. It was a tall, erect creature, well over two meters in height, covered in shaggy white fur. Its face was a sleek gray mask streaked with black; the features were not human. It blended so easily into the snowy air and white surroundings that it seemed to appear from nowhere. Ryne approached it closely, but could not determine whether the white fur was a garment or the creature's skin. He was startled when it spoke.

"Who?" the creature asked in the starfarer's common tongue.

"Troopers of the Sternverein. We seek men like ourselves," Brocmal responded. The creature made no reply. "We seek other men from the stars. Men like us," Brocmal said again.

"No men. No men like us. Gaorod here," the creature said in a grating voice unsuited to human sounds.

"No gaorod. Evil men. We seek the evil men. Lead us to them," Brocmal said.

"Go. No bad men. Go," the white creature said. At the last word he turned and fled into the blowing snow, and in an instant was gone from sight.

Certain unpleasant facts became immediately clear. Several of the fugitives had survived and settled among the Hingwoldin, and their place among the natives was exalted. *Gaorod* was a term to indicate someone godlike. These giants were not going to deliver up their gods to strangers; there would be a battle. The ease with which the creature had appeared and disappeared in complete silence was disconcerting. They would be dangerous foes.

Brocmal acted at once. The Hingwoldin's visit indicated that the fugitives were likely to be in the nearby village. The best plan was to strike at once, before they could move out and the Hingwoldin could organize an attack. He split the force into two groups, to hit the village from both sides. Strike time was two hours by the chronometer.

Ryne remained in Brocmal's party. As they drew closer to the village, a Hingwoldin suddenly appeared in their path. Ryne could not tell whether it was the same one they had seen before, but when it spoke, he knew it was another.

"Go back. The gaorod stay, and you must go," it said, gesturing forcefully.

"No gaorod are here. Only false gaorod. Evil men. They kill others and steal their goods. We come to punish them," was Brocmal's reply.

"No! No!" the Hingwoldin repeated. It gestured again, more violently, and roared like a beast. Brocmal raised his pistol and stood his ground.

Shots came, and then shouting. The creature vanished, and the noise from beyond the village grew louder. Brocmal signalled his troop forward. They charged the village and entered it unopposed. Once again, they found a deserted village, but in this one the signs of hasty departure were everywhere.

Posting half the men to hold the village, Brocmal took the rest to join the other party. Their leader, Over-lieutenant Hortt, called out the good news.

"We got them all, Commander! They were sneaking out along a back trail, and they walked right into us," he announced.

"All of them? Are you sure?"

"Every one listed, Commander."

"Did you have to kill any Hingwoldin?" Brocmal asked.

"Three. They tried to protect their gaorod, and we had to get them out of the way. The rest just disappeared."

"I've seen that trick of theirs, and I don't like it. We're heading back to the *Blesser* right now, before those white giants start appearing all around us," Brocmal said.

He gave the order, and they moved out at once. Clearly, this was a time for speed. The mission had been completed successfully, without a single casualty. By pressing hard, they could be at the *Blesser* in under three days. The faster they moved, the less time the Hingwoldin had to avenge the slaying of their gods.

They skirted the village, and made their way through the pass and across the lake without incident. Snow was falling heavily now, but the trail was clearly marked. They entered the thick wood, and here began the long nightmare.

The attack came without warning. One moment the troopers were marching in a staggered double column, making good speed despite the thickening snow. Then, suddenly, men were falling, ripped by razor-sharp lenticular missiles that came from nowhere, made no sound, and struck with deadly accuracy. The troopers opened fire at once, laying down a curtain of fire on both flanks, and the attack was abruptly over.

Seven blackjackets lay dead, killed instantly. Six more were badly wounded. No one had seen even a single attacker.

A second attack took three more troopers just as they came in sight of the first village. Again, the Hingwoldin struck and disappeared without revealing themselves.

The snow ended as they reached the village. Here they spent the night, with a double guard alert to every sound. But there was no attack. As the light broke, they set out again. Their way led through heavy forest. It was hard going; some of the wounded had to be carried. When the snow began to fall again, every man expected to feel one of the lens-shaped missiles at every step of the way.

The Hingwoldin struck again and again, each time picking off more troopers, reducing the party to a handful. But now they began to grow overbold and impatient. They showed themselves in the open, when no falling snow concealed them. What a trooper could see, he could shoot. And what he shot did not attack again.

Ryne was rear guard of the diminished group, glancing behind him and all around, but seeing nothing. Then, out of the corner of his eye, he caught a glimpse of motion among the trees. Diving forward, he fired. The others took cover at once. Something hissed past his head, and a Hingwoldin screamed and staggered toward him. Ryne rose to one knee, took aim, and fired a second shot directly into the creature's chest. It went over backward and moved no more. Ryne let out a long breath. No other humanoid he had ever seen or heard of was able to stay up after being hit at that range by a Sternverein bullet.

He went to the fallen Hingwoldin and tugged the weapon loose from its grip. It was a green stick, about a meter long, slotted at one end to receive a lens-shaped missile. Ryne tucked it into his belt and took one of the missiles. A shallow biconvex chunk of some glassy material, razor-edged, it barely fit into his open hand. They would want to study these on Occuch, he was sure.

The last attack came at the edge of the forest. Snow had begun to fall once more, and visibility was poor. All was still for a time, with no sound but the labored breathing of the troopers and the crunch and squeak of their boots through layers of snow. Then the fury erupted.

Missiles came from all sides, and more men went down. But the Hingwoldin showed themselves in strength at last. The blackjackets no longer fired into empty whiteness: now their enemy was before them, swarming from all sides on the slayers of their gods. They came on, heedless of the fire that cut them down, ready to die *en masse* in one final act of holy vengeance.

The snow was churned up all around, blotched with blood and gory foam. Ryne stood at the center of a palisade of corpses, ankle-deep in bloody muck. He felt as though he had been in this place for days, fighting without letup, and still the creatures came on. But at last it grew quiet. He fired at one writhing white giant, then waited. Nothing came at him. Something moaned and stirred, and then was still. It was over.

Brocmal was dead, nearly decapitated by a missile. Hortt and one of the Over-sergeants had been killed in the first attack. Both Under-lieutenants were dead. The second Over-sergeant and both Under-sergeants had been picked off along the way. Forty-one Hingwoldin lay dead around them, and Ryne could not guess how many more had crawled into the forest to die of their wounds.

Six blackjackets remained alive. All were wounded. All had sustained damage to their cold-climate suits. Ryne brought them back. He carried and dragged the worst wounded, drove the others on with threats and curses and blows, and did not rest until the *Blesser* achieved the drivespeed transit.

His face, hands, and feet were frostbitten. The jagged end of a broken throwing stick had worked its way into the wall of his intestine, and he had severe internal injuries from a struggle with two of the creatures. Heavy stim dosage had left him with a palpitating heart and violent muscle spasms.

The *Blesser's* medical officer was a corpse on a mound of bloody snow, and the survivors were too weak to help Ryne. The three guards, all recruits, gave him first aid, and put him into full stasis. They could do nothing more. His only help was on Occuch.

CHAPTER 12

Ryne survived the Hingwoll mission without loss of limb. His injuries required extensive surgery, but the battle-surgeons of Occuch were experts. He recovered in good time.

For his actions he was breveted Under-lieutenant and awarded a second Combat Star and the Order of Leddendorf. After his convalescent leave, which he spent at the Rehabilitation Compound on Occuch, he reported to the Advanced Training Camp. He found himself a considerable celebrity in both places, and was often called upon to tell the story of the Hingwoll run.

At this point in his career he was assigned to his first marriage. It came as something of a surprise. Ryne knew that the Sternverein arranged marriages between suitable personnel, and expected to be assigned to marriage one day, but not so early in his career. His bio-subjective age was only twenty. Clearly, this assignment was an indication that he was doing well in the eyes of his superiors.

LIKE the vast majority of his comrades, Ryne accepted the Sternverein's marriage policy without question. He had known of it since training days. Now and then he met someone who voiced reservations, but he paid little heed to them. They were sentimentalists. They would not last long as black-jackets.

It was hard to understand objections. The Sternverein marriage assignment was the only reasonable solution to a number of problems.

An ordinary marriage was impossible for a black-jacket on space duty. Because of the drivespeed timelag, a starfarer aged at a slower rate than a planetbound companion. The phenomenon was not fully understood and seemed to vary widely in its manifestations, but it was an indisputable fact. The spaceways abounded in sad tales of homecoming to aged offspring who had forgotten even the name of the parent who returned to them still in the prime of life. The Sternverein would not permit a loyal trooper to suffer such a blow.

Even more important, the Sternverein needed proper recruits for the Security force. Old recruiting methods were no longer sufficient. As the mission of the Sternverein grew ever more complex and delicate, often the children of proven veterans were the best candidates for the program. Assigned marriages assured the Sternverein of a source of pure-blooded troopers who could be trained to loyalty from birth.

Nolo, assigned marriages—both served the Stern-verein's grand design. Nolo had eliminated the sexual tensions of extended space voyaging once and for all. Thanks to Nolo, discipline on the white drive-ships of the Sternverein was always at peak, and emotional distractions were eliminated. The policy of assigned marriages provided a controlled, constructive outlet for the occasional release of emotion, while avoiding permanent bonds that might interfere with duty. For duty came first, as all in the Sternverein knew. That was the oath they had sworn, the words they lived by. It left little room for gentler feelings.

Between training cycles, Ryne was sent to the Rest Center to meet his assigned partner. He arrived early, and found himself with an entire day on his hands. Ordinarily, a free day at the Rest Center was highly prized, but Ryne was impatient for this one to end.

On the medico's advice, he had delayed the Nolo scrub to the last possible moment. He completed it only one day before his departure for the Rest Center. Now he was assailed by unfamiliar sensations. The experience was not unpleasant, but it was slightly bewildering. He felt like a man remembering long-forgotten dreams. He was newly experiencing commonplace sensations with an intensity that astonished him. It was like a heavy stim dosage, but far more pleasurable.

He smiled at everyone who caught his eye. Some smiled back, and greeted him, even if they were total strangers. Others looked at him coldly and walked on, but he was not offended. He understood. They were on Nolo.

Ryne walked for hours, enjoying sights, sounds, and smells. He was constantly on the brink of being overwhelmed by all that was happening to his senses. Music filled the air, and bright colors were everywhere. The Rest Center was built on the shore of the Sea of Demetriou; the sea breeze bore a sharp and stimulating scent he had never noticed before. He inhaled deeply, savoring each breath, and memories stirred deep within him.

Suddenly he was hungry. It was not the hunger of a space run or the training camp. That was only the reaction of a machine demanding fuel. This was different. His mouth watered. He longed for tastes and textures and aromas long forgotten. At once he corrected himself: not forgotten, but ignored. Nolo had not dulled his senses. It had redirected his attention to keep him alive. But now that was all behind him for a time.

He stopped to dine at a place overlooking the red sands, where the sea breeze blew and light danced merrily on the water. The sight reminded him of Jadjeel, long ago. Unexpectedly, he felt moisture gathering in his eyes, and he raised a hand to wipe them dry.

"You've been on Nolo for a long time, trooper. I can tell that right away. Go on, let the feelings come out. That's why we have a Rest Center," said a voice close at hand.

Ryne looked up, blinking, and saw a tall, slender man, heavily bearded, with a pleasant smiling face. He was an older man, and he seemed kindly and very wise.

"It's my first time off Nolo," Ryne confessed. "I'm still a little. . . . I guess I'm not used to emotions yet."

"They all say that the first time back is the hardest. But you'll get over it soon, and you'll feel wonderful."

"I feel pretty good right now. Everything here is so nice, it's as though everyone wanted to make me happy."

"We do, son. That's what the Rest Center is for. Anything you need, anything you want."

At the moment, Ryne wanted to talk. The tall man listened, a look of interest on his face. "I was remembering my homeworld. It's called Jadjeel, far off toward the Cohannan Densities. Even the white ships seldom go there. But it's a beautiful planet. Bright skies, open seas, a comfortable climate most of the year. Even Deadlands has a kind of bleak beauty. It can be a dangerous place to cross, but if you're prepared, the night skies are worth all the danger. I've never seen the stars so bright on any world as they are in Deadlands at night. And the sea, when the sotal fleet is returning. . . ."

His voice choked in a rush of emotion, and he stopped. The tall man laid a comforting hand on his shoulder. "It's good to remember, sometimes. But don't forget that Occuch is homeworld now. This is your home, trooper, right here with us. We're your people. You go out to the stars and risk your life for us, and we don't forget it. I'm Siad, the director here. I'll see to it that you have whatever you want."

"Thank you, Siad. My name is Ryne."

"Well, Ryne, I think you'd feel a lot better if you had someone to talk to—and I don't mean an old groundling like me. A young fellow like you ought to have a companion to share all these wonderful memories. I can get you any kind of companion you want. We have them from all worlds."

"Yes, I'd—no! No, I can't, Siad. I have a companion!" Ryne blurted. He was completely befuddled.

Siad looked puzzled. "You entered alone."

"No, not here, not yet. I'm meeting her. I've been assigned a marriage. We're meeting at third watch."

"In that case, my congratulations, trooper. And since you won't be wanting a companion, let me offer you something else—if you're just off Nolo, you must have an appetite like a snargrax. Let me order you the best meal we have."

"That's really why I came in, Siad. But I don't know anything about food."

"You don't have to, son. You just trust us."

Smiling to reassure him, Siad left Ryne and entered the main building. Ryne trusted him completely. The blackjackets had nothing but praise for Rest Center directors. Their duty was to make sure that every blackjacket who entered their facility had everything he wanted, when and how he wanted it. The best directors seemed almost capable of reading a trooper's mind and anticipating his requests. Ryne had wanted a feast, but did not know how to go about ordering. He was unaware of the names of most planetary dishes. But the director would see to everything. The Sternverein took care of its own.

The first dish arrived almost immediately, a bowl of green fruits the size of his thumbnail. They were sweet and delicious. No sooner had Ryne finished the last one than the bowl was whisked away and a fresh one brought to him, this containing a rich spicy paste studded with crisp kernels. Next came a plate of sweet golden spirals, crackling hot. Dish followed dish, each more delicious than the one before. Ryne savored sweet and sour, soft and crisp, hot and cold, spicy and bland, in every combination he could imagine. Every dish pleased with its own unique savor, and yet nothing sated. He was ready for each new taste, his palate as fresh as if every dish were the first. After the golden spirals he sipped the cool sweet wine of the midlands. After the seventh dish came the bitter red of the mountains; after the tenth, a frosted goblet of Stepmann green. When he had consumed the last morsel of the fifteenth and final offering, a tiny glass of quachoote, the dark blue liqueur of Oba Minor, was placed before him. He was left for a time in silence and solitude, to enjoy the experience in peace. Then the director reappeared.

"Are you pleased, son?" he asked earnestly.

"It was delicious, Siad. I've never eaten like this before."

"I'm glad we made you happy. I hope you'll come back to visit us with your companion. It would honor us to serve you again."

Ryne left shortly after. Second watch was nearly over, and he did not want to be late for his first meeting with the woman assigned to be his wife. Much as his mind was drawn to imaginings of her, he found it hard to keep his thoughts from the meal he had just eaten. He had never tasted anything as good as those strange foods, never drunk such liquors. He was not aware, of course, that his digestive system was operating naturally for the first time since his Nolo treatment. Even the most ordinary food would have tasted rich and flavorsome to him now. Nor was he aware of the tranquilizing anti-aggressives that were mellowing his disposition. He knew only that he was happier than he had ever been before.

The goodness of the Sternverein astonished him anew, as did his own good fortune to be a favored member. His eagerness grew, and anticipation urged him on. He hurried through the busy streets of the Rest Center to the rendezvous.

HER name was Keela. She was the most beautiful, most desirable woman Ryne had ever seen. She was, quite literally, Ryne's ideal mate, as he was hers. The Sternverein had matched them carefully long before either one had been notified of the impending marriage.

He did not know how to greet her properly. Formal terms of address and rank seemed out of place, but he could think of no others. He felt foolish and awkward, more like a clumsy boy than a decorated space veteran. When at last they were alone, he started to apologize. Keela stopped him at once.

"We musn't begin with apologies, Ryne," she said gently.

"But I feel so stupid, Keela! I feel as though I'm doing everything wrong!"

"It's always that way after Nolo. Everything will come back to you, Ryne. I know. It's happened to me before."

He looked into her eyes—wideset eyes, deep brown, of a softness that drew him to her—then he forced his glance away. "There isn't much to come back, Keela. This is the first time I've been off Nolo. You're the first wife I've ever had."

She smiled and raised a soft hand to stroke his cheek. "But you've had companions, haven't you? Well, I'll be like a companion, only we'll be together for a longer time. And we'll have children for the Sternverein. They want us to."

Ryne hesitated, then asked, "Will we be happy?" He was not sure whether this question marked him as a fool, but he felt compelled to ask.

"We'll be very happy, Ryne. We'll be together from now on, just to make each other happy. You'll see." She opened her arms to him and he pulled her close. She was soft and warm and yielding, and all his uncertainty vanished in her closeness. Everything came back to them very quickly.

THEIR trial period together was a blissful time. Before it ended, both Keela and Ryne had declared their willingness to continue the marriage for full term.

When they returned to Ryne's camp, their possessions had been moved into new quarters, which were unlike anything Ryne had ever seen. The walls were not unbroken white, but covered in colors and delightful patterns. The furniture was soft and relaxing. Sweet, pleasant music played unobtrusively all through the day, and a vidscreen was available whenever they chose to watch.

They often watched it together in the evenings. The shows were different from the violent prismatics provided at the camp, or on space runs: tales of love and jealousy, of powerful emotional conflicts happily resolved. They always ended in scenes of reconciliation and love-making, and both Ryne and Keela found their own feelings stimulated by the actions on the vidscreen. The people of these prismatics were people much like themselves.

For a time, Ryne could not accustom himself to experiencing everything with this new intensity. His laughter was too loud, and tears came too easily. Keela, too, experienced the difficulty. She had had an earlier marriage, but that was in the past. She had since been on a long space mission, and was freshly off Nolo. But she and Ryne worked hard to channel their drives into constructive action.

With all the strong feeling they experienced, however, they never quarrelled or grew angry. They could not have done so. In their situation, anger would have been a counterproductive emotion, and so it was suppressed by additives in their diet, just as more appropriate emotions were stimulated. There were some who knew of this practice, and accused the Sternverein of drugging its members into obedience. But the Sternverein ignored the charge. Its members were not drugged. They were merely subjected to induced physiochemical alterations in the interests of the organization. Had they been informed, they would have accepted gladly; therefore, there was no need to inform them.

KEELA had been on three Second Contact missions. Her work was delicate, very difficult, and essential to the Sternverein mission. Ryne listened to her for hours, absorbing knowledge that would supplement his Alien Cultures interest, which he still pursued. She, on the other hand, had only the basic combat and survival skills. With Ryne's coaching, she soon rose to the level of expert. That was the ideal of a Sternverein marriage—a strengthening and sharing of skills for the good of the entire organization.

They had both heard stories of the old ways of marriage. They rejected those ways, as they rejected the foolish customs of some worlds. For outsiders, marriage often meant the forming of a new unit, separate from all others, to pursue selfish goals. Keela and Ryne spurned that. It was isolation—a kind of death. For a member of the Sternverein, only one unit existed. To draw apart from it was to leave everything. The only good marriages were those that recognized this truth.

No one had ever stated it explicitly. It came from no tape or prism, no oath or teaching. But all knew that it was so, and was the basis of their lives: the Sternverein was more important than any member or group of members.

It was clear to Ryne that this was the way it had to be. Individuals had doubts. They hesitated, and sometimes they did not act at all. When they acted, they frequently did so on insufficient data and later regretted their action. Individuals made errors, left important work undone, or wasted time and effort in foolish pursuits. Individuals were weak. The Sternverein was wise, and strong, and decisive.

Ryne found it good to have someone like Keela to talk to frequently. When he told her how he hoped one day to become part of a Special Options force, like Varyssa and Thone, she understood. Special Ops were the elite of the Security branch. But she made Ryne see his own role in the blackjackets in a new way. He was as valuable to the Sternverein as any Special Op. None of them could have performed the deeds he had performed. There was a job for everyone in the Sternverein, and the Sternverein always chose the right person for the job. And Ryne was reassured, and much encouraged, by her words.

He sometimes told her things he would not have dared to say to anyone else. As he remained free from the influence of Nolo for an extended period, he found himself with thoughts that disturbed him deeply. Keela was sensitive to his moods, and one night she asked him what troubled him.

"I've been thinking about my missions, Keela," he said.

"I often remember my missions. It can be very satisfying to think back on the good work you've done," she replied.

"No, that's not what I mean. You were on Second Contact missions. I've been on three nemesis runs. They're very different."

"We all do the work of the Sternverein."

He grunted a half-hearted reply and fell silent. She moved closer, laid her head on his shoulder, her hand on his chest. "You're unhappy, and you must tell me why. That's why we have each other, Ryne, so we can grow and improve with one another's help. What is it about your missions that troubles you?"

He could not hold back. "I wish we hadn't killed those Hingwoldin, Keela. That's all. I think about that planet, and I wonder if we did something wrong."

"You told me they tried to shelter renegades. That condemns them automatically, according to the Court of Mercy."

"I know that. But maybe they shouldn't be condemned like that. Maybe we should have tried to explain things to them before we took final action."

She sat up facing him and looked at him sternly. "Ryne, they attacked troopers on a mission. They killed members of the Sternverein."

"But first we killed three of them. You see, Keela, they were deceived. They thought those fugitive pirates were gods. When we came, they tried to protect their gods. That's a *good* thing to do, isn't it?" He looked anxiously into her eyes, needing her help and wisdom.

"I'm surprised to hear you speak like this," she said. "You're a Mechanist. You know the laws of purpose and dysfunction."

"Of course I do, Keela, but then. . . ."

"Repeat them," she cut in. "What is the purpose of the individual?"

"To seek to know and fulfill his or her proper function," Ryne recited.

"And what about dysfunctions?"

"Dysfunctional components are to be located and eliminated."

She placed her hands on his shoulders and looked intently at him. "Ryne, you've been talking about *killing*. But you're a blackjacket. You don't kill. You've never killed anyone yet, and you never will. Your purpose is to locate and eliminate dysfunctional components, and you do it superbly well. You're a good man, Ryne—you know your purpose and you fulfill it. That's why I love you so much."

He pulled her close, kissed her, and buried his face in her soft, sweet-smelling hair. "Keela, I love you," he whispered. "You're so wonderful. You *understand*."

She was right, of course. The doubts that lingered in his mind were foolish, and would soon pass. He forgot all in the passion that possessed them both.

THEY were together for eleven months, GSC, and Ryne found them the happiest months of his life. Keela was everything to him—his lover, his comforter, at once his pupil and his teacher. Their marriage was a beautiful paradox—he experienced greater turbulence and greater peace during this time than he had ever known before, all thanks to Keela. She was a perfect companion.

The day came when Keela and Ryne reported to the Medical Compound together and said their last goodbye. Ryne was put under Nolo once more, and left soon on a nemesis run. Keela remained behind.

The return to a Nolo state came as a surprising relief. He had been remembering too much, thinking troublesome thoughts, feeling too deeply. Emotions could give great pleasure, but they could also cause pain even worse than the pain of combat wounds. Now, once again, Ryne could be detached and calm. The cold barrier of Nolo and the sustaining importance of the Sternverein mission made life so simple: duty was all. Obedience and loyalty solved all problems. He began to understand why so many old-timers chose to stay on Nolo until expressly ordered off. It made things so much more bearable.

Upon his return, Ryne was informed that Keela had given birth to twins. As was the policy, he was not told their sex. Indeed, it was a mark of great favor to have been told that there were two children. He was very pleased.

IN THE course of his career, Ryne was assigned to other marriages. He and his partners provided the Sternverein with a total of seven acceptable recruits, a creditable record. All the marriages were good, but for some reason, Ryne never thought about the others with as much pleasure and happiness as he did about his time with Keela.

He saw her once, much later in his career, at a diplomatic function. He was married at the time to a Third Contact methods' analyst. Keela had been on space duty to far systems, and looked scarcely older than she had in their days together. He caught her eye and nodded to her. She appeared to be still under Nolo. She gave no sign of recognition, and so he made no attempt to speak to her. It was better that way, he told himself.

He said nothing about it to his wife. Afterwards,

alone, he laughed at his moment of weakness. He was becoming a sentimentalist, that was clear. It was lucky for him that the Sternverein kept him too busy to be brooding over the past. Thank the blazing rings for Nolo!

CHAPTER 13

Dumabb-Paraxx was an interesting world, but one not often visited. It was sparsely populated, the site of colossal and enigmatic ruins, home of a single humanoid race, the Quespodons.

The chief differences between Old Earth humans and Quespodons were in the large bone structure and comparative musculature of the latter. Quespodons were short, stocky people, completely hairless, with pale skin mottled in patches of blue and purple, stretched taut over knots of solid muscle. Their mottling patterns were unique as fingerprints. Physically, they were perhaps the strongest race in the galaxy; but their mental powers did not match their physical strength. Despite a brain capacity of 1.163 Old Earth standard on the SRC scale, the average Quespodon was on the mental level of a child. There were the usual rumors of mutants, and of off-world Quespodons with brilliant intellects; whether the stories were true or not, such oddities were not to be found on Dumabb-Paraxx.

This combination of strength and weakness had led some galactic races to join in urging restrictions on the Quespodons. Clearly, such people were unfit to organize and manage a world; otherworlders were brought in to do it for them. Their emigration was seen as a danger, and forbidden. The Quespodons raised no objection to these measures, but the possibility of opposition was always present. A close watch was deemed advisable. The obvious choice to police the planet was Sternverein Security, and so a base was established on Dumabb-Paraxx. To this base came Ryne, now an Over-lieutenant, in command of defense and security.

He was received graciously. While his Under-lieutenants supervised unloading, Ryne was conducted directly to the Base Commander's suite and seated comfortably on a mound of small, soft cushions in the welcoming area. The base stood on a high plateau, and the Base Commander was in the tallest building. His suite was sparsely but tastefully fitted out, more in the style of a successful merchant than that of a Sterverein Security officer on duty. Ryne felt awkward here, as if he were seeing a comrade in an unguarded moment. To divert his attention, he looked out at the broad sweep of plain, the chief city, and the titanic ruins that loomed beyond them. The vista through the glass wall was impressive indeed.

The Base Commander and his orderly entered the room. Ryne started to rise, but the commander waved him back to his seated position. After a gesture to his orderly, he settled opposite Ryne.

"Be comfortable, Over-lieutenant. You'll find that possible even on Dumąbb-Paraxx," he said.

"Thank you, sir," Ryne replied. At a quick appraisal, the Base Commander appeared to be almost excessively comfortable. He looked soft, out of condition. His attire was not the regulation uniform, but some colorful robelike garment.

"We'll have some refreshment. My name, by the way, is Sunden, and you needn't address me as 'Sir.' I'm an Over-lieutenant like yourself."

"The name is Ryne."

"I must say, Ryne, your youth comes as a surprise to me. I believe you're the youngest Over-lieutenant I've ever seen."

"I started early. And I've been mostly on space duty. Nemesis runs. Rank comes fast."

The Base Commander gave a sigh. "Only to some. How many nemesis runs, Ryne?"

"Six on the *Blesser,* two on the *Spurr,* and two on the *Elidur*. Three turns at the training schools on Occuch, in between times."

Sunden appeared genuinely impressed. Ryne turned to the panorama that unrolled beyond the glass wall.

"A splendid view from here, don't you agree?" Sunden said proudly as he took two goblets of the very best Stepmann green from the orderly and handed one to Ryne. "Your suite is next to this, so you'll have much the same prospect before your eyes during this assignment."

Ryne sipped the wine. "A pleasant thought. Will I really have nothing to do but look out my window?"

"Oh . . . you'll have to take an occasional stroll through Cosparaxx, just to see what our spotted friends are up to. I suppose you'll have to visit the working camps now and then. And I'm sure you'll want to tour the ruins. They're most impressive."

"I've been looking forward to that. I spent all my spare time en route studying the prisms on Dumabb-Paraxx. The only place you'll find structures like these ruins is on a quarantined world."

"And neither of us desires to do that," the commander assured him with a look of distaste. "Tell me, Ryne, what is your own theory of their origin? Who built these incredible structures?"

"The First Travellers. That's the only theory that makes sense."

"Yes, of course," Sunden said thoughtfully. "Lately, there have been stories circulating in Cosparaxx . . . foolish stories, but troubling, in a way."

"What sort of stories?"

"Well, quite preposterous, really. I feel silly repeating them. It seems some of these Quespodons have come up with the idea that the ruins are not the work of the First Travellers, but of the first Quespodons. Or perhaps they believe the two are identical. It's hard to tell *what* they think." Sunden shook his head and shrugged.

"Quespodons are trying to claim credit for those?!" Ryne asked. When Sunden solemnly nodded, Ryne burst out, "Blazing rings, Sunden, those ruins are the products of a civilization surpassing anything we know! The first Old Earthers to see them were astounded, and they had come from the most advanced technology in the galaxy. And the Quespodons are trying to say that *they*? . . ."

"I realize the absurdity of such a claim, Ryne. I mention it merely as a curiosity. Nothing of any importance."

Ryne set the goblet down and took a hard new look at Sunden. The Base Commander might be soft and slovenly from long assignment to this outpost, but he was not a fool.

"Do you believe someone is stirring up the Quespodons?" Ryne asked.

"I doubt it would be possible for anyone or anything to stir up such creatures. They don't seem capable of dreaming up such a tale themselves, but, of course, one never knows with halfwits like these. We do know that they're easily led. They believe anything they're told often enough. After all, we implanted an entire cosmogony on this planet in a single generation, and now they believe it's their own age-old mythical history. Someone might conceivably be trying to implant a new cosmogony."

"Why?"

Sunden sipped his wine and gazed at the glass in silent thought. Abruptly, he said, "I have no idea. I've told you, Ryne, this is all idle speculation. Don't take it so seriously. Dumabb-Paraxx is a quiet world. There's little for an intelligent man to do but think, and one's thinking tends to become either fanciful or convoluted. Or both. To a man who's accustomed to the brutal reality of a nemesis run, my ideas may sound. . . ." He waved his hand in a vaguely deprecating gesture and turned to Ryne as if in apology. "Perhaps my most recent Nolo treatment was not fully effective. I suggest we discuss something more sensible."

"I'd like to hear your theories," Ryne said.

"If you wish. But really, Ryne, you're making a great deal out of nothing. Let me suggest that you take the day to settle in, and this evening you and your staff be my guests for dinner. We'll talk more easily then."

Sunden's softness was beginning to show again. He

had a good mind, perhaps, but his will badly needed strengthening. Ryne elected to push his point, but make it appear a compromise.

"Tell me your ideas now, as briefly as possible," he said. "I'll have the day to think them over, and tonight I may be able to ask intelligent questions instead of simply sitting and listening."

"As you wish." Sunden pointed to the half-empty goblet, but Ryne shook his head. The orderly refilled Sunden's goblet, and the commander said, "First possibility: the Sternverein have an enemy somewhere, and that enemy is seeking out our weak spot before making his move. If it were to be shown, for example, that we are incapable of maintaining order on Dumabb-Paraxx, we would lose credibility among the races who look to us for protection. Those who now fear us might grow less fearful. And so this enemy—or his representatives, or his agents—would like to see the Quespodons turn on us. Arousing their dormant racial pride is the first step."

"Assuming that their pride is roused, are we vulnerable?"

"The estimated population of Dumabb-Paraxx is two hundred million. Otherworlders number six hundred ninety-seven. Less than half that number are Sternverein personnel capable of strong resistance. In view of the odds, we are indeed vulnerable." Sunden replied coolly.

"All right. Go on."

"Second possibility: the stories are true. Those ruins are all that remains of some ancestral civilization that has somehow declined to what we know now as Quespodons. I have no idea how they learned of it. Perhaps racial memories, too deep to be completely forgotten. There are analogues on several worlds. Even on Old Earth, there were legends of prehistoric giants, and an Age of Gold."

Ryne nodded. "And this, too, would serve to rouse racial pride."

"True. But in the absence of extra-planetary manipulation, we could control the situation. We might even turn it to our advantage."

"I agree. What's your next idea?"

Sunden sipped from his goblet before replying. "Third and final possibility: a mutation. We know that Quespodon brain capacity far exceeds Old Earth standard, yet for some unknown reason it had never developed. Perhaps now, development has begun." He gestured lazily to the scene beyond, spilling a bit of wine. "Out there may be one, or two, or a hundred, or perhaps a million Quespodons with minds superior to ours. They see us restraining their people, siphoning off their strength for our own use, denying them the stars."

"Your third theory is the most dangerous."

"Dangerous? I'd say deadly, Ryne. Fatal. If they were simply an angry mob being manipulated by otherworlders, a bit of bloodshed would soon cool their ardor. But led by their own brilliant leaders, the Quespodons would be unstoppable."

Ryne's jaw stiffened. He knew the word was not intended as a challenge, but he could not let it pass. "Nothing in this galaxy is unstoppable except a black-jacket, Sunden. We might lose a battle, but we always win in the end. Always."

"Of course. I spoke loosely. Please remember, Ryne, I'm only speaking of an imaginary situation. Don't act as if there were really a danger," Sunden said.

"Did you transmit this information to Occuch?"

"And be ridiculed as a dreamer or a fool? Certainly not, Ryne. Investigate, if you choose, and report what you like. But I have no intention of becoming the laughing-stock of Occuch by crying for help at the first ridiculous rumor I hear."

"Do you know how long the rumor has been circulating?"

Sunden looked at him innocently. "I have no idea. The management teams and exploitation groups knew nothing of it. When I mentioned it, they looked at me as if I were raving. I have no spies among the Quespodons, no private sources of information, Ryne. We have as little to do with one another as possible, the Quespodons and I, and we're all happier that way. You're the first designated defensive man on the planet."

Ryne bit back the scathing comment he would have made; no point in alienating the Base Commander at their first meeting, even though the man was a lazy, self-indulgent weakling. This would go in his report, and proper action would be taken at the proper time. There was no place in the Sternverein—not even on Dumabb-Paraxx—for an officer who shirked his duty.

RYNE spent the early part of his assignment inspecting the defenses. His discoveries were not comforting. If the Quespodons were indeed being goaded to the point of rebellion, they would have an easy time of it. Every otherworlder camp on the planet, even the Sternverein base, was vulnerable. Ryne found feeble strands of wire that even the weakest Quespodon could snap between his fingers; firing positions that could hold back a disciplined army, but would be useless against a tide of flesh that paid no heed to losses; an attitude of careless disdain for a potentially dangerous enemy. Ryne observed, taped, sketched, and struggled to pull the defenses together in time.

He had two bright young Under-lieutenants with him. Ritho was a first-rate engineer, Gerian a nemesis run veteran like himself, who had become an expert, though reluctant, administrator. They met to hear Ryne's report and instructions.

Ryne gave the full situation report, then plunged ahead. "We start tomorrow. Ritho, you're in charge of the construction. Gerian, you see to it that Ritho has all the manpower and material he needs. The Sternverein base gets first priority. I want a ditch five meters wide and five deep, with a sloping outer wall. Everything you dig out goes to build the inner wall. I want it all faced with stone and finished smooth as glass. Firing positions every three meters along the top. If they hit us in force, that will buy us enough time to lift off. Once the base is done, you start on the outposts."

"It's a shame to plan on running," Gerian said unhappily.

Ryne turned on him sharply. "We're talking about a massacre, Lieutenant. If we don't run, this base will be wiped out. If this base is wiped out, the word won't get back to Occuch. Another of our ships will land, and more of our comrades will be massacred, because we didn't warn them. Don't go looking for ways to be brave. They'll come."

"I only mean—with all respect, Sir—that we might be able to turn them back."

"Study your Cultural Groupings prisms. Gerian. This is a one-race planet. Close bonding and strong revenge motivation against otherworlders is the normal pattern. Our top kill potential is less than one-tenth of one percent of the population. We don't stay to fight, we lift off. Predicators agree."

"About the manpower, Sir," Ritho asked tentatively.

"What about it? We're on a planet full of muscle. We'll use the Quespodons."

"If they suspect that we're building defenses against them, there's sure to be sabotage."

Ryne sighed wearily. "Don't you know how to lie, Lieutenant? Tell them we're building a reservoir, or an algae farm, or that we're reconstructing some of their ruins. You can say we're building a temple for their Over-being, Keoffo. Or a hospital, or a wind-funnel, or a pleasure complex. Anything you like, as long as it's plausible. Just be sure to clear it with me."

When the conference was over, Ryne left the others and started for his quarters. The night was clear and cool, and the base was brightly lighted. He looked up, but could see no stars beyond the glare. Sunden's voice close by startled him.

"If you're looking for the Chained Man, Ryne, you'll have to step out of the light."

"I wasn't looking for stars. I've seen better constellations than these. Just stretching my neck muscles."

"You've been working hard ever since you arrived. 'Too much sharpening weakens the blade,' you know. You could do with a day off."

"Too many people have taken too many days off, Sunden. There's work to be done. Perhaps when the defenses are finished."

The Base Commander sighed. "A pity. Your third month on Dumabb-Paraxx and you still haven't seen the ruins."

"I'm here to improve defenses, not inspect ruins."

"The first Travellers built well, Ryne. You might learn something from them about constructing defenses. And the way passes through Cosparaxx. If we stop there to dine, and we meet the local leaders, there's no telling what you might hear. They're very careless talkers, you know."

Ryne had no choice but to accept the invitation.

THE ruins of Dumabb-Paraxx were indeed magnificent. Having ridden through the streets of Cosparaxx and seen the dreary stretch of one-story buildings that made up this world's major city, Ryne was almost moved to laughter at the thought that those who built and lived in those rude huts would dare to claim kinship with the master architects who had dreamed these structures. But all thought of laughter vanished in the presence of the ruins. They were overwhelming even in their decay. Broken domes, crumbled ramps, and truncated spires drew the imagination of the beholder to fill in the lost glories. Vast constructs enclosing vast spaces, curving steps to nowhere, were enough to silence Ryne. He knew something of the races in the galaxy, and their history, and he knew that none could boast of anything like this. Not even the Old Earthers had built for all time.

From behind him, softly and elegiacally, Sunden's voice whispered:

Gleaming crystal towers rising on the mountains,
Flashing in the sunlight, glinting under stars;
Sparkling water rushing, dancing in the fountains,
Cooling breezes blowing through the busy bright
*   bazaars.*

He did not move. Words and voice were perfectly suited to this time, this place. They spoke the feelings Ryne could not share, and he listened, fascinated.

Feet upon the highroad, faces in the city,
Laughter and low voices in the quiet of the night;
Hands that offer welcome, eyes that offer pity,
Arms that offer comfort and a promise of de-
*   light. . . .*
Now the glass is shattered, now the stone is
*   broken,*
Now the metal twisted by the thoughtless force
*   of time;*
All the ways are empty. Word no more is
*   spoken.*
Emptiness is ruler and the silence is his token,
Ruling in a ruin where the ageless shadows climb
Over broken fragments in the aftermath of time.

They rode back to Cosparaxx in silence. At the outskirts of the city, Sunden said, without preamble, "I heard that recited on my homeworld and never forgot it. My father said it was made long ago by Alladale, the great anthem-maker."

"About this world?" Ryne asked.

"About every world, sooner or later."

THEY spent that night and the next at a clean, drab inn near the center of Cosparaxx. Ryne thought it best to meet all the local dignitaries on a single trip, to avoid unintentional slight to anyone. He found the Quespodons quite respectful, eager to please, and totally worthless as a source of information. He was careful to mention the ruins in every conversation, repeatedly expressing his admiration for their creators. His efforts produced no results. If there were Quespodons who believed that their remote ancestors, and not the half-mythical First Travellers, had built those structures, Ryne did not meet them, nor did he meet anyone who spoke of them.

He returned to the base puzzled, but undeterred. Work on the defenses continued, and Ryne drove the workers hard. The troopers could expect no breaks from him. He considered the base personnel badly out of condition through their commander's negligence, and his own men stale from a long space run. Everyone worked to full capacity, Ryne included. Even Sunden became visibly more attentive to his duty. Ryne began to have hopes for him.

The time passed quickly and uneventfully. There was no sign of an uprising, or even of mild unrest. The Quespodons were as peaceful and placid as ever. Ryne found himself bored and impatient to be done with this fruitless assignment.

Thirteen months of his sixteen-month GSC tour of duty were gone before the daily routine was broken by the arrival of an unexpected visitor. At the end of the long dry winter, a dented, ill-tended, much travelled Second Stage tramp cruiser locked into place on the base's auxiliary landing ring.

The appearance of the driveship proclaimed the owners. Ryne was not surprised to learn that they were a trio of free traders, claiming the landing right under an old Sternverein protocol. He greeted them with mixed sensations. Among the troopers, free traders were known as "free riders," or worse. They took the protection offered by the Sternverein, used its facilities, and gave nothing in return. They were resented, and their arrival could mean discipline problems. But free traders were a good source of information. Even the most hostile worlds gave them access, and Ryne had found them as willing to sell their observations as their goods.

Sunden was quick to invite the trio to dinner on the evening of their arrival. Ritho was on duty at a remote outpost, but Ryne and Gerian joined them. It was an unexpectedly pleasant evening. The traders' last stop had been on Gerian's homeworld, and so the young Under-lieutenant did much of the talking. Ryne was content to let him. He welcomed the chance to study the traders.

Their senior, who did most of the talking, was of the Old Earth line, though a sorry specimen of it. His name was Pollgon Hoctor. A paunchy, sweating man, quick to agree and even quicker to apologize, Hoctor typified to Ryne the glib, ingratiating way of the free traders. They take the money, we take the risks, was the troopers' perennial criticism of such men. Ryne thought it justified, and was annoyed by Sunden's excessive courtesy toward the trio.

The other two were different. Ryne had never seen their like before, and they puzzled him. They were bigger than he, and heavier of frame. The taller was well over two meters, the other not much shorter. They wore loosely-wound headcloths of gaudy striped material and the long robes common among dwellers in hot dry lands. But they were of no desert race known to Ryne. Their blunt, open features and pale rust-colored skins were not those of a desert people. Ryne combed through his memory, but could find no clue to their origins. Puzzled and slightly annoyed by his ignorance, he bided his time until dinner was over. As they withdrew to the welcoming area, he engaged Kaber, the taller one, in conversation.

"Don't think me rude, Kaber, but I'm curious about your homeworld. Where are you from?" he asked.

Kaber gave a soft deep laugh and pointed beyond the glass to where his ship stood. "That's my home, Over-lieutenant. My parents were in partnership with old Pollgon long before my birth. My brother and I are starbrats. We were born on the *Renascence* and we've spent most of our lives aboard her."

"Odd name for a driveship, *Renascence*," Ryne observed.

"One of my forebears picked the name, not I," Kaber said pleasantly.

"Tell me, where did your forebears come from? I've been to a score of worlds, and I've studied cultures. I thought I knew every race in the galaxy, but I've never seen anyone like you and your brother. I hope you don't mind my asking. . . ."

"Certainly not, Over-lieutenant. After all, you're the defense officer. You'd be remiss if you were not curious."

"Call me Ryne, please. I'm glad you understand."

"I do, Ryne. I only wish I could be more helpful. You see, my family have been traders for at least six generations, and bloodlines become rather complicated in that time." He laughed again, and went on, "My parents introduced me to relatives on every world we touched, and no two looked alike."

"Whatever the mix, it turned out well," Ryne said. "We could use a thousand like you in the blackjackets."

"High praise, Ryne. Very kind of you. We respect the security troopers, and are grateful to them, but I'm afraid you'd be disappointed in us." Kaber touched the cloth that wound around his head and covered his neck. "As you see, we are followers of the Ninefold Law. Violence is forbidden to us. Thus, we are traders, not fighting men."

The trio departed shortly after, pleading work on shipboard. Ryne observed their walk and doubted their claim to a peaceful way of life. Hoctor scurried anxiously before them, but Kaber and his brother walked with the cautious grace of experienced fighting men. Of course, it was understandable. Even a free trader had to look after himself from time to time, and few got through their travels without a minor altercation here and there. Ryne decided to keep an eye on the traders. He was not suspicious; merely curious. As Kaber had said, that was his duty.

The traders took quarters in Cosparaxx, and one or two of them remained there each night. For a time they seemed to follow a fairly regular rotation, but then, after twelve days on the planet, the brothers took to spending several consecutive days at a stretch in the city while old Hoctor returned to the ship alone after dark. Ryne observed this for a few nights and then decided to investigate their doings more closely.

He was too tall to pass for a Quespodon, but by night, dressed in a walking cloak and hunched over, he was able to wander the sparsely-peopled ways of Cosparaxx with no more than an occasional curious glance. He kept to the shadows, responding to salutations with the gesture of greeting but saying nothing.

The two brothers were not at their inn. Ryne set out to find them. He knew his way around the city by this time. He covered the outer streets quickly, walking toward the center, checking for signs of unusual activity, gatherings, anything out of the ordinary.

He felt good. After the long drudgery of defensive work at the base and outposts, and polite snooping in the city, it was exhilarating to be on a lone stalk once again. His long-barreled pistol was tight against his chest, knife and shortsword by his side, all within easy reach should need arise.

In truth, he anticipated no need for weapons. There was no reason to suspect that Kaber and his brother were involved in anything questionable. And besides, Ryne was a blackjacket; he walked where he chose, when he chose; armed or unarmed, among enemies or friends, in light or darkness. Here on Dumabb-Paraxx, he was the bringer of law, the arm of justice. He was a ruler, and the Quespodons knew it. There would be no trouble.

As he approached the great market, Ryne saw the first sign of activity where none should be. The market was filled with stone enclosures of various sizes where merchants and traders met on the appropriate days to conduct business. By night, and on off-days, these trading sheds were empty. Now and then a wanderer might sleep in one of them for a night, but wanderers were infrequent on this world.

Tonight the market was busy. Ryne saw lights moving about among the sheds and figures converging on the deserted area. Here was something to investigate. He walked down one of the narrow lanes, keeping to the shadows, and closed in cautiously on the area where he had last seen light. He saw two other figures, both Quespodon. Neither showed a sign of having seen him.

Their goal was one of the larger sheds, a low, flat-roofed building about twenty by thirty meters. It was not used for trading, but served as an eating-place for the marketgoers.

After first looking about cautiously, Ryne watched the two Quespodons enter and knew that something was afoot. Whether Kaber and his brother were involved or not, the situation demanded investigation. He decided to enter. There had been no challenge to the others, no countersign asked or given. Admittance seemed easy. Exit from such places was often more difficult, but Ryne thought the risk worthwhile. He was well armed. If trouble were to break out, he would have better odds in a closed space, with a corner to protect his back.

The building contained about forty of the small cruciform dining benches used by Quespodons. But instead of facing one another, the assembly of some two dozen were seated so as to face the short wall opposite the entry. Kaber stood atop one of the benches; he was addressing the crowd.

Ryne took his place on an empty bench, a few paces from a corner. His entrance went unnoticed by all. He hunched his shoulders and kept his hood well forward to conceal his face.

At first, Kaber's words were meaningless. He did not speak in the common tongue, but in a deep mellifluous singsong, to which his hearers responded at regular intervals. When Kaber switched to the speech of the Quespodons, Ryne was able to gather enough to realize that he had come in on some sort of religious ceremony. He felt foolish and rather disappointed. But he remained.

Kaber finished speaking and gave place to his brother. Ryne waited until he was gone. Seeing that it was permissible to leave before the others, Ryne rose and made his way to the doorway. Kaber was waiting outside and greeted him warmly.

"We appreciate your concern, Ryne, but it is unnecessary. The Quespodon are a tolerant race, and we are safe. Quite safe," Kaber said. "I regret any inconvenience we may have caused you."

Ryne had not expected to be recognized so easily. He tried to conceal his surprise under a brusque manner. "Quite all right, Kaber. We are responsible for your safety under the protocol, you know."

"True. But if I had any idea that Commander Sunden was concerned, I could have assured him, and saved you an evening's work."

So Sunden knew about this. That was interesting to learn. Ryne made some further non-committal remarks, and Kaber suggested that they return to the base together. On the way, he explained his presence in the building.

"During our business dealings, we learned that some of the people of Dumabb-Paraxx are followers of the Ninefold Law. They are few in number, and feel isolated. My brother is a full Gatesman, and I am a Mound-warden. We felt bound to aid our fellow believers, and your Base Commander was most sympathetic. I had no idea he feared for our safety."

"It's customary to protect all visitors. Quespodons are an unpredictable bunch. I'm surprised your religion admits them."

"The same Maker made all," Kaber said simply.

"So I've heard. He did a poor job with this lot, though, if you'll permit me to say so."

"You are not a believer, then, Ryne?"

"I'm a Finite Mechanist. Most troopers are."

"It is a cheerless creed, Ryne."

"This is a cheerless galaxy. It suits."

Kaber laughed his deep, patient laugh and changed the subject adroitly. Ryne had more questions to ask, but he was not able to steer the conversation as he had hoped. They returned to the base by a long route, and Ryne was winded when they arrived. But despite this and the lateness of the hour, he went directly to Sunden's quarters.

If he was annoyed, Sunden did not show it. He listened to Ryne's story, pondered his questions, and bluntly replied that he had been fully aware of the brothers' activities. Since they presented no danger to Sternverein interests, he had seen no need to inform Ryno.

"They might have been doing something far more dangerous than howling a lot of prayers, Sunden," Ryne said.

"Indeed? What might they have done?"

"They might have been feeding the story about the ruins of Dumabb-Paraxx being he work of early Quespodons to anyone who wanted to listen. Did that never occur to you?"

"They might have been saying any number of things, Ryne, but in fact they were celebrating the Ninefold Law. I believe you saw and heard them. Do you doubt the testimony of your own senses?" Sunden asked mildly, following his question with a yawn.

"I know what I saw tonight. They've been at this for a lot more than one night, though. Kaber is a clever man—a lot smarter than he wants us to think. I might have been seen, and this all done to deceive me—to deceive us all."

"You're a very suspicious man, Ryne."

"I'm responsible for the defense of this planet, Sunden. I want to question those three traders very closely."

"Do whatever you like, Ryne," Sunden said airily.

"They're no different from the other traders who stop here."

"Do the other traders stay in Cosparaxx for days, too?"

Sunden sighed. "Of course they do. Do you expect us to have a parade of Quespodon merchants wandering across the base to conduct business on a free trader's driveship? Really, Ryne."

"All right, you think I'm making too much out of this. Maybe I am, and if I am I'll admit it. But the situation here. . . ."

Ryne stopped abruptly at the look of astonishment that transfigured Sunden's face. He followed Sunden's gaze beyond the glass to the ring area, and then the high whine of a drivecoil made him grimace. The *Renascence* was lifting off.

When the sound died, Ryne turned on Sunden. The man paled and shrank back before the cold glare. He began to stammer a reply, but could not speak coherently. With a moan, he collapsed on the cushions by the window.

Ryne felt a sense of revulsion. "You're relieved, Sunden. I'm assuming command of the base under emergency procedures. You can explain it all back on Occuch," he said.

CHAPTER 14

A Sternverein board of inquiry heard the whole story. By the time the board was convened, Sunden had recovered his self-possession. He seemed to be seeking not so much to defend himself as to charm the members of the board.

Ryne, he told them repeatedly, was a very valiant and dedicated young man, but perhaps not quite ready for the responsibilities of a planetary defense officer. After all, he had been trained to obey, not to think; to act, not to plan. It was only natural for him to see the danger of a planetwide uprising in the slightest departure from routine. The fact remained that there had been no uprising. Dumabb-Paraxx was still safely under Sternverein control. For his part, Sunden said magnanimously, he did not want to see a promising young officer's excellent record marred by a disciplinary decision. He only urged that in future, Ryne be assigned to duties more suited to his competence.

Ryne argued bluntly from the facts, emphasizing the danger to Sternverein interests on Dumabb-Paraxx. In his judgment, the base and outposts had been threatened; as defense officer, he was obliged to take action to assure their safety when the regular commander did not.

After he and Sunden had made their statements, the advocates stepped forward to represent them in the inquiry. Ryne followed the proceedings with understandable interest, but as the days passed, he grew dissatisfied and confused. What was being said and done in the magnificent black and silver chamber, within walls laden with a century of battle trophies, with the crest of Leddendorf looming over all, seemed to grow ever more obscure. It had less and less to do with Ryne and Sunden, more and more to do with the advocates, the board itself, and issues Ryne could not grasp. He felt dwarfed by some immensely com-

119

plicated phenomenon that no one would explain to him.

In growing frustration, he abandoned all attempts to follow the proceedings and instead turned his attention to those present. It was most enlightening.

Ryne had come to the inquiry in the traditional trooper's dress uniform. On his tunic he wore a single decoration, the Order of Leddendorf, rather than the baldric displaying all his honors. There was no point in showing the others. A man who had won the Order of Leddendorf had no need to prove himself further. But in the surroundings of the chamber, Ryne's appearance was almost austere.

Everyone else, Sunden included, was wearing a colorful non-combat uniform and displaying every decoration imaginable. And as Ryne's knowing eye went from baldric to baldric, he perceived the truth and his hopes faltered. These gaudy gentlemen, assembled in all their finery to judge his action in a time of danger, had never seen combat. They were weighted down by a different kind of honors.

The commonest decoration of all was the Order of Unity, given for long service. It was to be seen on every member of the inquiry board. Few of Ryne's comrades had won it, and few expected or cared to. A decoration given merely for growing older in safety was not highly valued by fighting men.

Nearly as frequent was the bright badge of the Sword and Tower, awarded for advancing the interests of the Sterverein. And the Hexagon of Tressander, for organization and planning; the Six Red Stones, for diplomatic achievement; the Grand Cordon, for meritorious service; the Collar of Almagaid, for territorial administration. And along with these were the Order of the Seal and Mirror, the Order of the Thorn, the Banner of Nal, and a score of others, all bright and colorful adornments to uniforms bedecked with epaulets and cuffs, braid and capelets. All, in Ryne's eyes, were worthless. Not one award for combat. Not one for wounds. Not even the simple golden triangle for space duty.

He was being judged by men like Sunden, not like himself. They were speaking to one another, and not to him or about him. His case was inconsequential, merely an opportunity for them to parade the trinkets gathered in planetbound comfort, strut in uniforms more suited to a Trulban throne room than a gathering of troopers, and bandy their jargon back and forth —the clever language of men who spend their life at desks. He felt a great loathing for them, and for what their presence here meant to the Sternverein. Only Nolo restrained him from stronger feelings.

After this moment of insight, Ryne wanted only to get the whole degrading business over with and return to the clean, uncomplicated ways of space, where men like these did not go. When his advocate, after a lengthy speech too rarefied and elegant for Ryne's understanding, suggested the chance of an honorable compromise, Ryne accepted it without question.

In the end, the solution was no solution at all. Sunden was placed in command of a secure trading base where defense questions would never arise. Ryne was assigned to the Special Training Program as a Cultural Groupings tutor pending a command assignment on the next nemesis run. No one was rewarded, no one was punished, nothing was decided. Ryne felt that he had participated in a great sham.

He took a few days to relax at the Rest Center, but found it difficult to put himself at ease. He did not elect to undergo the Nolo scrub, even though it was overdue. The thought of coping with full, undamped emotions was enough to discourage him. Even his surroundings seemed to conspire against him. He remembered first meeting here with Keela, and felt disgust at the thought that she might now be sharing marriage with one of the spangled popinjays from the inquiry board. Everything was going bad, even his memories. The Sternverein was no longer a place for fighting men. It had become a home for talkers and well-dressed gentlemen. Not for Ryne, or his kind.

He stopped in an Ease House, picked out a dark corner, and ordered a bottle of coldfire and one mug. The director sent over a pretty little Malellan, but Ryne told her he was fresh from space and still on Nolo. He wanted solitude and oblivion.

He was still on his first mug of coldfire when an elderly trooper came to his table and greeted him by name. An Over-sergeant, with skin like leather and cloud-white hair, the newcomer wore an old-style uniform like Ryne's. Ryne studied him in the dim light, puzzling over half-remembered features. They were familiar, but he pictured a younger version, a boy, a recruit on his first run—then he knew that it was Herril, from the *Blesser*. They ordered another bottle and another mug, and sat down to talk of old times.

Herril had lost both legs on his fourth nemesis run. Prosthetic treatment had been the best, but he was not judged up to space efficiency. Since that long ago day, he had been Personal Weapons Master at the Advanced Training School. He told Ryne his whole story, and concluded, "It could have been worse, but I miss the stars. Look at me, Ryne. We were kids together on the *Blesser,* and now I could pass as your grandfather."

"I'm close to a century old, GSC," Ryne said.

"And bio-subjective?"

Ryne sipped his coldfire before replying, "Twenty-nine."

"I'm sixty-eight. That's what happens when you're stuck planetside," Herril said gloomily. "I would have taken anything, any rotten menial slot, just to be out there. But they wouldn't approve me."

"You could resign. A former blackjacket could get good work as a guard on a trader or a pilgrim ship. Good pay, and you're in space."

Herril looked at him in disbelief. "No one quits the Sternverein. You can't do it, Ryne."

"Maybe I'll find out." Ryne refilled his mug with care and added, "I'm thinking of getting out myself. Maybe we could hire out together."

Herril slumped back, disbelief on his weathered features. "Even if it were possible, Ryne, why would *you* quit? You're the best we've got!"

"Thanks, Herril. But there are a lot who don't agree."

"You mean the board of inquiry?" Ryne looked up sharply at the words, and Herril waved his hand deprecatingly. "We know that kind, Ryne, and we don't much care for them. They're a pack of rutupis."

Despite his low spirits, despite the Nolo, Ryne had to smile at the perfection of that image. A rutupi was a small arboreal creature of Occuch, noisy and ill-tempered, covered with thick fur in a dazzling pattern of stripes and spots. It always sought the highest branches, and flung its excrement down on any of its kind who came too near. When attacked by a larger creature, it played dead.

"The rutupis are running things now," Ryne said.

"The Sternverein is growing, Ryne, and it's changing as it grows. When you're on space duty, it's easy to get the feeling that things are changing too fast. Come back from a long space run, and there's a whole new generation running things."

"It's a pretty poor generation."

Herril gulped coldfire and shook his head. "No worse than some that have gone before. We're moving into a whole new phase now—all the old-timers know it—and some are trying to turn it to their own advantage. Men like you have got to stay in, just to keep the rutupis from taking over."

Ryne grunted. "I can't get out, and they've taken over already. So where does that leave us?"

"They haven't, Ryne. That hearing scared them. We all saw that. If you quit the Sternverein, you'll be making them stronger. You're the youngest Over-lieutenant in the blackjackets now. Soon you'll be a Combat Commander. They can't hold you back."

"They don't have to. Nemesis run commanders don't last long. They just have to send me out enough times and one time I won't come back."

Herril looked very wise. "Pretty soon there won't be any more nemesis runs. I've heard the word, Ryne, and I believe it."

"What's the matter? Is the Sternverein running out of men with guts? I'll go out alone, if I have to."

Herril laughed. "We're running out of enemies, Ryne. It took three centuries, but the message got through: if the blackjackets come after you, they find you. And when they find you, they kill you. No exceptions. Don't forget, the predicators have a tracking accuracy of ninety-nine percent now. We've fulfilled Leddendorf's first objective."

"And now?"

"I don't think anyone knows. I've heard rumors, though."

"What kind of rumors?"

Herril looked about cautiously before speaking. "Well, some people are saying that a way has been found to get the Old Earth weapons onto driveships without having them blow up."

Ryne exhaled audibly. "That would change everything."

"It would. Stay with us, Ryne. Maybe you can make sure the Sternverein goes the right way."

RYNE stayed. He remembered his conversation with Commander Kurtessus, and their talk of the days when the primary mission had been accomplished. In Ryne's lifetime, the commander had said, and he was right.

What would the blackjackets do now? Would they be healers, builders, colonizers? Perhaps now there would be time to study and learn the secrets of the galaxy. Ryne had visited a score of worlds, but knew nothing of them. He had come to hunt, and kill, and leave. But that first world . . . despite the predators, it could be colonized. And Diundran . . . the pirates, all Otherworlders, had succumbed to disease. Why were the natives unaffected by the Gathan sickness? There was valuable knowledge to be gained. Even the ferocious Hingwoldin might yet be made allies. Certainly, there was much work ahead.

Ryne led two more nemesis runs and was decorated for bravery on both. He enjoyed two good marriages. Then he was sent on a mission to the world called Mog Korb, and what happened there changed his life forever.

PART THREE

MOG KORB: THE RENEGADES

CHAPTER 15

The Mog Korb mission was a routine Third Contact. Its chief purpose was to arrange a trade agreement, its secondary purpose to prepare the Korbians for Sternverein membership.

The Korbians had behaved in a manner both friendly and receptive since their first encounter with otherworlders, and had shown no aggressive characteristics. But much was still to be learned about their ways and their world, and the Sternverein did not send traders and negotiators to unfamiliar planets without protection. Ryne was guardian of the mission. He was charged with a double responsibility: to safeguard against any threat from the Korbians and to prevent any aggressive act by Sternverein personnel.

The latter possibility seemed remote. To avoid even the suggestion of a threat, the mission had been kept to five members: three men and two women. Only Ryne and his aide, Under-lieutenant Walgan, were blackjackets. The others were from the non-combat branches.

Ryne had other duties as well. As a gesture of Sternverein trust and goodwill, he was to place his knowledge of defense and security methods at the service of the Korbians. Once the planet became a member, it would be expected to join in the common defense and would in turn receive any support it might require.

He was also under confidential orders to evaluate the aggressive and defensive potential of the Korbians. Should they elect to remain outside the Sternverein, they were a potential enemy.

Ryne spent most of the long run to Mog Korb in the ship's information center. The Second Contact mission had gathered a mass of material on the Korbian language, customs, and history. He spent nearly all his waking time mastering the contents of the tapes and prisms. When he was not busy in this way, or when he needed a break from his studies, he familiarized himself with the ship.

From the time he had seen her poised on the ring on Occuch, Ryne had felt strange sensations about this ship. She was a beauty, the pride of the Sternverein's white fleet. But for Ryne, she bore a heavy freight of memories. The Mog Korb mission was aboard the driveship that Ryne had helped take as a prize on his first nemesis run. Refitted and renamed, she was now the *Kurtessus*.

On an inbound voyage, with a successful mission behind him, Ryne might have been tempted to dwell on his memories of those early times. But now he was far too busy. Besides his sessions in the information center and his responsibility for shipboard security, he was in charge of the training schedule. Of all those aboard, only he and Walgan had any proficiency in weapons. And however peaceful a planet might appear, the Sternverein expected even its non-combatants to be prepared to defend themselves. Mog Korb was on the fringes of the known systems, and the trip was long. Even so, Ryne had no time to spare. Before the voyage was well under way, he had scheduled supplementary training sessions for every fourth watch. He and Walgan supervised.

After one of these sessions, in which both of his pupils had managed to score something near respectability on the firing range, the three of them conversed over mugs of scoof. The others were relaxed, and Ryne himself was reassured by their improvement and more than usually cordial. He did not like the Mission Secondary, a small, strutting man named Omrand who reminded him of those gaudy gentlemen promenading in the corridors of the fine new buildings on Occuch. But the man was doing his best on the range, and Ryne did not wish to discourage him. The other member of the trio was the Mission Primary, a science advisor named Locrin. She was smart and capable, and Ryne considered her a good choice for mission commander.

Omrand sighted down his arm and aimed a finger at an imaginary target on the bulkhead. "You've brought it all back, Ryne. I haven't fired this well since training days. You've had experience as a trainer, I can tell," he said importantly.

"I've served at the training schools on Occuch."

Locrin said, "You must have been a good trainer."

"I was the best they ever had," Ryne said. He was not boasting, merely passing on information.

"I don't doubt it. Tell me, Ryne, wouldn't you rather be back on Occuch, training promising recruits, than star-hopping with a crew of merchants?" Omrand asked.

"We're not all merchants. Locrin's a scientist, and Walgan and I are security men. And you and Angusel are more than just merchants."

"Yes, of course, but my point is that we're traders and negotiators. We're going out to talk, not to fight. It doesn't seem like your kind of mission."

Ryne sipped his scoof and set the mug down. His face was expressionless. "I didn't pick it. I was assigned, so I'm here. *Someone* must have decided that it's my kind of mission."

"I think I know why Ryne's along," Locrin said. "Everything seems to indicate that the Korbians are totally non-aggressive toward outsiders. They'll need an expert to teach them how to get their planetary defenses up to Sternverein standards."

Omrand grunted. "*If* they join."

She looked at him disapprovingly. "Do you still believe that they won't join the Sterverein when they're offered membership?"

"They might not."

Locrin turned to Ryne. "I hope you don't take such a negative view of our mission."

"I don't understand why the Korbians wouldn't join the Sternverein at their first chance. They're an intelligent race, but without technical development. We can give it to them. What puzzles me is why we're so anxious to get them in," Ryne said. "What's on Mog Korb that interests us?"

"The planet is rich in some very rare metals. More important than that, it would be our outermost base. Mog Korb could open a whole new sector of the galaxy to us," Locrin said.

Omrand went on, "If we install twenty or thirty landing rings, we can make Mog Korb as important as Occuch."

"There are other worlds out here," Ryne pointed out. "If the Korbians don't join, we can bypass them and find another base."

Locrin rejected that idea at once. "The other worlds are all uninhabitable. Even on the best of them, it would take all the resources of the Stern-verein to build a base and keep the personnel alive from one day to the next. No, Ryne, we need Mog Korb and we want it soon. I think the natives will go along."

"Omrand doesn't agree, though," Ryne said.

"Don't overstate my position. I think the natives will see what's best for them eventually, but I wouldn't be surprised if it takes a lot of convincing on our part. The Korbians have some strange cults and beliefs. The Second Contact team was able to learn that much, but very little more. They don't talk about their beliefs to otherworlders. Suppose they all believe that there's some religious law forbidding them to join us or let us use Mog Korb as a base?"

Ryne sipped his scoof and said, "We could try to convert them."

"I doubt that that would work. And of course, force is absolutely forbidden," Omrand said.

Ryne nodded. "Too bad. It can be very helpful."

"With five of us?" Omrand was sceptical. "That's all we are, and only two are blackjackets."

"I had a trainer back on Occuch. Seadhal was his name, a Thorumbian. He used to say we wasted our strength sending out thirty and forty man groups on nemesis runs. 'One planet, one blackjacket,' he used to say. 'That's all you need.' So we have good odds."

"But we will not use force," Locrin said firmly. "We'll just have to do the job without it."

CHAPTER 16

The *Kurtessus* locked in the ring on Mog Korb at dawn on a bright warm day. Ryne was first on the ramp. He stood at the top, just outside the port, and looked over the world that lay before him. Coming to a world on which he had no enemy felt odd. Mog Korb seemed a good planet.

The sun had just cleared the horizon on his left. Clusters of domed dwellings shone half-alight; one side glowed with color, while tails of darkness coned behind. The sky was brightening, the air was cool and fresh, and the scent of growing things drifted on the morning breeze. Even under the palliative of Nolo, Ryne felt a sudden brief stirring within him as his senses reacted to the unexpected beauty of the scene. But the feeling passed quickly, and he started down the ramp alone.

The Korbians were gathering before he reached the ground. He knew what to expect, but even so, their appearance surprised him. Except in a few minor details, they resembled all the representations of Old Earthers he had ever seen.

There was no possibility of prior contact. Old Earth lay halfway across the galaxy, and this world had never been visited before the first probe by a Sternverein Pioneer team. The Second Contact group, upon close examination, discovered differences in organ placement that ruled out the possibility of direct descent. Indeed, the Korbians, despite their appearance, were only .971 Old Earth on the Racial Cognate Scale. But Ryne was still struck by their resemblance to his racial forebears. If it were not for the ridges beside the eyes, and the deep twin grooves running from nostril to jaw, the resemblance would have been perfect.

In the morning light, the gathering crowd was as colorful as a flock of cirrindors at mating time. Their garments were all much alike in form, but no two were

133

similar in color or design. Men and women wore a knee-length kilt, with a simple sleeveless tunic or short cape over their shoulders. All wore low soft footgear of hide, decorated in intricate patterns. The capes and tunics and kilts were bright with color, dizzying in the variety of decorations and emblems and symbols worked into them. Ryne, in his traditional black uniform and gleaming black boots, felt out of place for a moment. But any feeling of strangeness was soon expelled by the enthusiasm of the Korbians' greeting.

Formalities had to be observed. These Ryne had studied. He was ready. Before a word could be spoken by the newcomers, the host had to offer welcome. And before the host could speak, a ritual had to be performed, for the men and women of the white ships were strangers to Mog Korb no longer. In the Korbian social structure, they were kindred. They knew the planet and its people, and were bound to their ways.

At the foot of the ramp, before he touched Korbian soil, Ryne halted and raised his hands in the gesture of safe return. A tall white-haired man in a cloak of blazing gold and red and green stepped forward from the growing crowd and responded with the gesture of welcome and shelter-offering; then he drew back while six Korbians embraced the newcomer. An old man and woman clasped him to them as a son. A young man gripped his arm in friendship, and a young woman embraced him as a lover. A girl and a boy stood by his side as his children.

The white-haired man stepped before the group and spoke. "We welcome our ship-brother to Mog Korb. When the last ship-kindred departed, their leader said that a white ship would return to us before the seventh transit of Mog Dir, and his word was true. Reclaim your place on our soil, and be with us long."

Ryne stepped from the ramp and placed his feet solidly on the soft green sward of Mog Korb. The white-haired man placed his hands on Ryne's shoulders and said, "I am Milam, your friend and guide for as long as you wish and require."

Now the ritual called for Ryne to speak, and he did so, accepting Milam's hospitality for himself and his companions. He was impressed by the dignity of this old man and his people. They might be a backward race by some standards, but by others, equally valid, they were as civilized as any race Ryne had ever met.

The preliminary ceremony was over, and the others were now free to descend the ramp and tread Korbian soil. Like Ryne, each was received by six Korbians in the kindred-ritual, and touched by Milam. When all had been properly welcomed, Korbians and visitors retired to the village to celebrate the return of the white ship and its ship-kindred.

Ryne had never lost his curiosity about the great variety of human life forms found among the stars. As a boy in Jadjeel, he had seen all otherworlders as brutal enemies until he met the two who saved his life and freed his world. An Agyari and a Mallelan were his first heroes; Seadhal the Thorumbian was the finest trooper he had ever known. Since his first space duty, most of his friends had been of the Old Earth blood, it was true. That breed was predominant on nemesis runs. And the nature of his duties put him in contact with only the worst of every galactic race. But despite all the experiences that might have led him to see every alien as a deadly enemy, the force of those early impressions was great. It had created a lifelong interest in alien races and cultures, an interest Ryne had pursued even when superiors gave him no encouragement. Now he was grateful for his long discipline.

A biologist might have listed considerable differences between an Old Earther and a Korbian. But to the eye, the two were nearly identical. It was this very similarity that made Ryne's first days on Mog Korb seem unreal. Korbians looked so familiar, and yet their ways were not the ways he knew. Whenever a familiar pattern began to appear, some twist or turn left Ryne facing a mystery.

Emotions were displayed openly, without shame; but Ryne never saw laughter. Generosity was highly esteemed. Yet certain items could never be given as gifts. They might be bartered for a few pebbles, or a handful of herbs, or a ritual gesture, but there had to be an exchange. If there was not, both giver and receiver were ostracized. Ties between generations were strong, as were the ties of family. All other bonding was voluntary; but once made, it was made for life. A friend or lover could never be disowned.

Korbians were hunters, but their quarry was chosen by some means no outsider could fathom; they were herdsmen, but they had been known to slaughter an entire herd and leave the carcasses to rot while they themselves grew weak from hunger. They tilled the soil, but some of their richest land was left untouched for reasons that could not be explained.

Their dwelling-places presented the first direct challenge to Ryne's curiosity. The tribe that housed the Third Contact team were called, in their own language, the Dome Builders. Their dwellings were simple domes of what at first appeared to be glass, opaque and brightly colored. Actually, they were made of mud, applied over frames of skin and poles that were removed when the mud dried. A second, glazing coat, made of a specially treated clay, was then applied inside and out. When it hardened, it was impermeable and as tough as steel. The interior was dry and well insulated. The domes lasted for generations and showed no sign of age. Ryne was impressed by design and use of material, but when he tried to analyze the planning of the domes, he found only confusion. The placement of entrances made no sense.

In the massive dome-complex constructed for the Sternverein team, the arrangement was simple enough. One huge central dome served as a common room and storage area. Five individual domes opened off the central area, and an opening at one end of it led to the settlement. But every other dome complex was laid out differently; no two were alike. In some, the central dome had no entrance of its own; in others, the peripheral domes opened to one another, but not to the central dome. Some of the outer domes had public entrances; some were completely sealed off. The Second Contact team had made fruitless inquiries. Ryne asked about these matters several times and was politely told nothing. After the fourth attempt, he decided to bide his time. The mystery remained a mystery.

Secretive as they might be in some matters, the Korbians were willing to speak endlessly about others. During the days of celebration that followed the team's arrival, Ryne heard the story of the creation of Mog Korb and the Korbians, of their sun and sister planets, no less than a dozen times. By the time the celebrating ended, he knew the legends by heart. He could recite the tale of Agmog, the Shapeless Gorger, who ate all that was and spewed forth the sun, Mogor Besim, which promptly burned him up. He had heard how Mogor Besim, in remorse, had in turn brought forth four daughters; only one, Mog Korb, survived. The three sisters, Mog Dir, Mog Goh, and Mog Chela, were all stillborn and forever barren. It was the tears of Mog Korb for her sister worlds that had created the first domes, and from them had sprung forth the first Korbians, seven in number, to be the parents of all things.

The stories were told to Ryne in perfect seriousness. The childlike faith of the Korbians was quite different from the cold formulations of the Finite Mechanist teaching. He wondered—he could not ask —if the show of belief were itself a part of the ritual. It did not occur to him until long after that he was being instructed.

The welcoming ceremony lasted for three days, an odd mixture of ritual and random. Each night, at the fall of dark, all activity ended and the people retired to their domes. The Third Contact team maintained a night-long guard in their central dome, but no one came near. On the second night, during Ryne's watch, there was a sound of movement outside. He woke his relief and went out to investigate. He saw no sign of Korbians, but at the far end of the row of domes, no more than a blur in the darkness, something slipped from shadow to shadow and disappeared in the direction of the forest. Ryne said nothing to the Korbians, but the next day, as the celebration resumed, Milam spoke to him. His manner was solemn.

"You were in grave danger in the night, Ryne. You should not leave the dome."

"What's the danger?" Ryne asked.

"The shaugarr is near," Milam said.

"That's an animal, isn't it, Milam?"

"The shaugarr is our most ferocious beast. It lives in the cold country, but when Mog Goh meets Mog Chela, all the shaugarr migrate, and pass over our lands. They are very dangerous at this time," Milam said.

"You're hunters. Can't you hunt the shaugarr?"

Milam was startled by the question, and Ryne realized at once that he had trespassed on a forbidden area of questioning. Before he could apologize, Milam recovered his composure and said, "When the Sisters have parted, the hunt will begin. Will the star-kindred share?"

"Walgan and I will come," Ryne said, pleased by this opportunity.

Three days later, Ryne returned to his dome, exhausted after a long ordeal of routine but absolutely essential post-planetfall duties. He found Milam waiting with a message by the dome.

"The Sisters are parted. The hunt is on," he said.

CHAPTER 17

They left the settlement before the rise of Mogor Besim and rode in the semi-darkness until they reached the seashore. Ryne had done little riding in his life, but his mount was tractable and he had no difficulty. Indeed, his saddle was so comfortable and the haxopod's gait so regular that Ryne found himself drifting off three times before they stopped by the sea for the morning meal.

Here Ryne had his first glimpse of the hunting party in full light. Besides himself and Walgan, there were twenty-six Korbians; the group was about equally divided between male and female. All wore the usual kilt and tunic, but the colors were not the bright reds, golds, and blues worn among the domes. These were hunting outfits, in striped and spotted patterns of brown and dun and forest green, worn for camouflage.

Korbian weaponry was simple. Each hunter carried from six to twelve metal-tipped javelins and a long curved blade. The blade was worn in a scabbard on the back, the handle extending above the shoulder opposite to the drawing hand. They could be brought into action very quickly.

Ryne and Walgan were in black field uniforms and carried the customary pistol, shortsword, and knife. As always, they had ration units for several days.

While the rest sat down to the meal of hard bread and fruits picked on the morning's ride, Milam settled beside Ryne with a bowl of spicy hot shing for each of them. He studied Ryne's weapons with concern, but said nothing. Ryne accepted the bowl. Shing had been tested by the First Contact team. It was safe to drink.

Milam turned to Ryne and said, "You and your ship-brother carry no javelins."

"We have other weapons, Milam," Ryne said, patting the handle of his pistol.

"All the ship-kindred carry such things. Will they stop the charge of a shaugarr?"

. "They'll stop anything." When Milam's look of concern only deepened into doubt, Ryne went on, "I've had to depend on this weapon for my life more times than I can count. It's never failed me yet. Haven't you ever seen one work?"

"No. The ship-brothers who came before did not hunt with us."

Ryne was not surprised. It was understandable caution in a First or Second Contact team. He would be the first one, then, to show the Korbians what a blackjacket was capable of doing with his weapons. "Not all of us are hunters," he said.

"But you are a hunter. That is plain to see."

"Yes. I've been a hunter for most of my life."

Ryne sipped from the bowl of shing and observed the others. They were finishing the fruits with which they had begun the meal. He had never seen fruit like it before. It was cylindrical, about as long as his forearm, but no thicker than his finger, bright red and banded in gold. Some who had eaten the last of their fruit portion were now starting to eat the bread.

Korbian bread was hard as a rock. The custom was to immerse it in shing until it softened to a chewy consistency, with a crust that still crackled under the bite. The bread absorbed the spicy flavor of the shing and gave off a tantalizing, pungent odor. Ryne inhaled deeply. The aroma was not unpleasant.

"You drink shing, but do not eat our food," Milam observed.

"I'd like to try it, Milam, but it's against orders. Shing has tested out safe, but most planetary foods are harmful to otherworlders. The Sternverein has lost men that way."

Milam seemed distressed by this information, but said only, "A pity. The others said the same, but I thought you might be different. Mog Korb has delicious foods to offer."

"If the taste is anything like the smell, they must

be very good. It's a long time since I tasted anything as good as your food smells."

"This is plain food. We are only a hunting party."

"Ship's rations are a lot plainer," Ryne said.

"Do you live all your lives on the white ships? Have you no homeworld, you and your ship-kin?"

"Some do, Milam, but I don't. I came from a world . . . well, I wouldn't even recognize it now. It was something like Mog Korb, if I remember correctly. I lived by the sea when I was young. Then some bad things happened, and I joined the Stern-verein. I just never went back." Ryne looked out to where the morning sun laid a flickering path on the calm waters. For a moment, he thought of Jadjeel and wished he could see it once more. Then he turned away and finished the last drops of shing. Milam was looking at him with that same worried expression.

That, at least, could be easily taken care of. One shot at a shaugarr and he would put Milam's mind at ease regarding the safety of his ship-brothers.

As they moved along the shore, Ryne fell in beside Walgan. The Under-lieutenant was riding alone, carefully observing the terrain and the Korbians.

"Have you noticed how they ride in pairs in open country, and use a staggered single file through forest, Commander?" he greeted Ryne. "These people are mighty cautious for a peaceful race."

"They could be worried about wild animals."

"That doesn't explain the camouflage. Still, it's possible," Walgan admitted. He did not sound convinced.

"The shaugarr is something worth worrying about. Milam is concerned about our safety. He was wondering if we'd like a few javelins, to protect ourselves," Ryne said.

"Javelins? What about our pistols? Is there some reason we can't use them?" Walgan asked quickly.

"Nothing like that. He's never seen a pistol used, that's all. First and Second Contact teams had no occasion. The Korbians seem to think our pistols are some sort of talisman. They doubt their value as a weapon."

"They'll soon think otherwise."

"That's what I want to talk to you about. As guests of honor, we get the first chance at the shaugarr. It has to go down on the first shot. Remember, Walgan, we're only on this hunt to show them the power of Sternverein arms."

"I won't miss, Commander," Walgan said.

"I don't expect you to. Remember, shaugarr charge head on. The head is practically all bone, so you have to wait until they lift their head, and aim straight down the throat. No tricks, no fancy shooting. Just kill fast and clean, so they see what our pistols can do."

WHEN they turned inland to follow a rising trail, Mogor Besim was at midmorning height. The forest was thick at first, but it soon thinned and the riding became easier. Visibility was still poor, and Ryne peered carefully around him. They were in shaugarr country.

The party split into four groups. The division was accomplished so quickly and smoothly that the others seemed almost to disappear before Ryne's eyes, leaving him with Milam and five others. His respect for the Korbians was increasing steadily. For the first time, he found himself thinking that despite their lack of advanced weaponry, they might be a hard enemy to defeat—as hard as the Hingwoldin. But this was no time to dwell on that.

Silence was now essential. Ryne knew the gesture-language well enough to follow Milam's instructions. They tethered the haxopods in a circle, facing outward, and left them to graze. These were good-sized grassland beasts, powerful and with sharp hooves, well able to defend themselves against a shaugarr; no need to waste a hunter guarding them.

The seven proceeded through the forest on foot. Ryne was as silent as the others. He was pleased to see that Milam noticed this and gestured to show his approval.

A sound came from ahead. It was not loud, and it stopped instantly, but Ryne and Milam exchanged a glance and conversed in rapid gestures. A big animal, possibly a shaugarr, was ahead and slightly to their left. Ryne estimated the range at about sixty meters, but had not converted this to Korbian measure before the sound came again, louder, and closing on them. No more doubt: it was a shaugarr.

Ryne checked his pistol and moved into position at the point of the hunting wedge. On either side, his flanks were guarded by javelins. He moved ahead, silent, cautious, hoping for a clear shot. The trees were young, the trunks slender, but they grew thickly on uneven ground. He would have to be fast.

It was over in an instant. Ryne saw the rush of motion before he heard the crashing. The shaugarr burst from a low thicket on his right, no more than ten meters distant. Still in his stalking crouch, Ryne swung smoothly and fired down the open throat. The beast jerked in mid-air as if at the end of a tether. It seemed to crumple and turned slowly, in the air, its long forelegs thrashing wildly, until it crashed to the ground at Ryne's feet and lay still.

The Korbians were stunned. A shaugarr seldom died so quickly from a single javelin, and the Korbians knew that few of them could have launched one so quickly and accurately at such close quarters. They were so impressed by Ryne's feat that they became careless, and the second shaugarr took them by surprise.

But not Ryne. Even as he looked down on the misshapen carcass and moved his boot back from the spreading puddle of blood that ran from the mouth, he realized that this was wrong. The beast had come from the right, near at hand, while they had been tracking something ahead on the left. This shaugarr could not have been in front of them.

As he turned to warn them, the second shaugarr

burst from cover. Milam saw it too late. He threw quickly, a poorly-aimed shaft that went wide. Ryne's shot caught the creature perfectly at the shoulder. It buckled, let out a shrill scream like the rending of metal, a horrible sound to come from a living thing, and clawing at the air, it landed on Milam, bearing him down and tearing at him in its final agony.

The shaugarr was dead before they reached it. They dragged it off their leader and Ryne knelt beside Milam to examine him. There was blood everywhere, but most of it was the animal's. Milam had protected himself as well as he could. His shoulder and upper arm were badly torn, but there was no serious injury.

Ryne gave him a shock preventive and set to cleaning his wounds, posting the others to guard against any further attack. They did his bidding without hesitation. With the blood and dirt cleared away, Milam's injuries looked less fearsome: one gash from the shoulder to just above the elbow, and three deep gouges in the shoulder itself. Ryne disinfected them and clamped them shut, then placed a clear skin-tight sealer over all. Milam looked on with great interest.

"This second skin you place over my injuries— how did you make it?" he asked, gingerly touching the shining film that lay smoothly over his shoulder.

"It's a bandage. It allows clean air to reach the wound and heal it, but it keeps out infection. I'll remove it in a few days. How does it feel? Any pain?"

"Some. Not much," Milam said. He started up and Ryne lent him a hand in rising. Once on his feet, the old man moved his arm, testing to find his limits. Then, picking up two javelins in his injured hand, he turned his attention to the shaugarr.

It was a huge beast, oddly disproportioned. The forelegs seemed too long for the body, and the hind legs too short. And yet the thing was fast and agile. Its head was massive, studded with thick knurls of bone. The eyes were almost invisible under a thick brow ridge that terminated in two hooked hornlike protuberances. Ryne considered this beast and was grateful for his pistol and his training.

"They seldom attack in pairs. But I should have been alert. The one that charged first was not the one we were stalking," Milam said.

"That occurred to me as soon as I shot it."

"Lucky for me. You saved my life, Ryne."

"The others would have gotten him."

"No. They cast four javelins. Three missed, and the fourth . . ." Milam kicked at the javelin sticking high above the shoulder of the dead beast. It came loose and fell to the ground. He looked at Ryne. "They would have killed the shaugarr, but first the shaugarr would have killed me. It was you who saved me."

Ryne considered this tough old man, and was impressed. Lying on the ground in the death grip of a shaugarr, he had the presence of mind to protect himself, and the self-possession to observe his hunters with a critical eye. Milam was quite a man; Ryne was pleased to have earned his gratitude.

Milam was interested in the way Ryne had killed the shaugarr. When Ryne pointed out the hole made by the slug's entry, the old man was incredulous. He protested, "This is only a small hole, Ryne. Our javelins do better. How can it kill? Where did all the blood come from?"

"Let's look at the other one. You'll see it better."

They stood in the blood-soaked dirt beside the first shaugarr and studied the fallen beast. It was a full four meters long from muzzle to the tip of the stubby tail. The broad red stripe running from shoulder to haunch was broken by an eruption of bloody flesh, shattered bone, and intestine where Ryne's bullet had emerged, tearing the right rear leg half off.

"It makes a bigger hole coming out," Ryne said.

Milam was silent for a time, then he knelt and laid his hand on the shaugarr's shoulder and spoke under his breath. Rising, he said to Ryne, "It is a bad way to die."

"They're all bad, Milam."

"This way is without dignity. There is no chance. It tears apart, destroys; it does not merely take the life. I fear these weapons of yours, Ryne. They are too powerful. Think what would happen if they were used upon a man!"

Ryne knew what happened, but he said nothing. Two of the young hunters drew their blades and began to carve the shaugarr. Milam drew Ryne apart to speak with him confidentially.

"We have a ceremony, Ryne. It means much to us," he began.

"I understand. I'll give you privacy so you can. . . ."

"No, Ryne, it is something quite different. When a hunter downs his first shaugarr, there is a ritual to be performed. But in your case, it might be dangerous."

"I would have thought the dangerous part was over. What's involved?"

"Certain words are said, then the hunter must roast the beast's heart and share the meat with his comrades. It is important to us that you do this, because you are ship-kindred to us. But you say that to eat the things of Mog Korb might harm you."

Ryne weighed the situation. Planetary food of any kind was expressly forbidden. But his mission was to befriend these people and win their trust. Their ceremonies were important to them, and his willing observance of a custom might sway them more than any words or promises.

He knew that the needs of a specific mission overrode a general ruling. Twice, when the alternative was starvation, he had been forced to subsist on planetary substances. It had not been pleasant, but he had survived. He knew the symptoms of food poisoning. Both he and Walgan carried field medical kits. The risk was real, but not excessive.

"Let's start the fire, Milam. I'll observe the ritual," he said.

The old man was obviously pleased. Ryne found the ceremony as bewildering as many other features of Korbian life, but went through with it willingly. The shaugarr's heart did not appeal to his taste, but it digested easily. To show his good will, he ate rather more than he thought wise, but when they started back, he still felt no ill effects.

On the long ride to the settlement, his mind went to other things. The Korbians seemed unaware of what the Sternverein Security troops were and what they did. Milam considered him a hunter—did he know what quarry Ryne hunted before coming to this world? The question troubled him. And that was odd, because he did not ordinarily think of such things while under Nolo.

Ryne was not poisoned by the meat. He felt no discomfort at all, then or thereafter. On the next hunt, a young Korbian killed his first shaugarr, and Ryne participated in the ritual meal with the others. This time it tasted better. After the hunt, he tried eating a bit of shing-soaked bread. It was delicious.

Ryne could not know it, but the shaugarr's heart had stimulated enzyme production. His digestive system was slowly returning to normal. And with this change came others, not yet apparent.

CHAPTER 18

For twelve days the newcomers acquainted themselves with Mog Korb and the Korbians. On the thirteenth day they met to compare findings and discuss future action. To Ryne's surprise, the others all seemed dissatisfied with their progress thus far.

Omrand was the unhappiest of the group. "Since planetfall, I've had exactly five private conversations with Milam," he complained. "The first four dealt with the birth of the Four Daughters and the tears of Mogor Besim and all the rest of that nonsense. Interesting enough in its way, to be sure, but of small value in establishing a common ground for trade negotiations. The fifth time we spoke, all I heard was praise of Commander Ryne, the mighty hunter of the shaugarr."

"Ryne saved Milam's life, Sir," Walgan said.

"So I've been told, repeatedly, and of course I'm pleased to hear that. It was a nice display of our weapons' superiority, and it puts the Korbians in our debt. All very well, and we're most grateful to the Combat Commander. But I must say, Commander Ryne seems to be monopolizing the time of the Korbian leader. If I'm to be successful. . . ."

"I've spent no time with Milam except at his invitation," Ryne broke in.

"I grant you that. The old man has taken a liking to you. But I'm here to work out a trade agreement. I can't do it if Milam and all his advisors are constantly off hunting with you, or showing you mountain trails or whatever else they've been doing."

Despite Omrand's growing irritation, Ryne remained calm. He had thought little of this man on board the *Kurtessus,* but had withheld judgement. Now, having found that he was as ineffectual as he was pompous, he despised him. "I'm here to convince the Korbians that the Sternverein can protect them, and I'm doing my job. If you can't do yours, don't blame me," he said.

Tertiary Angusel, the Alien Cultures specialist for the mission, quickly said, "You're doing an outstanding job, Commander, as we all knew you would. But you must understand our difficulties. The Second Contact team warned us that the Korbians are a very cautious people in making agreements. They consider a promise absolutely sacred, and so they're slow to make one. They want assurance that there are no surprises awaiting them, because even if they find they've been tricked, they're bound to honor their word. It's absolutely essential for our negotiators to have ample time to explain the treaty benefits to the Korbian leaders. Now, that's impossible if they're always off somewhere with you and Walgan, isn't it?" She looked at Ryne in appeal.

"You've got it wrong, Tertiary," Ryne said. "We're under no deadline. The negotiators have all the time they need. If I can get the Korbians to depend on Sternverein power and trust to it for their protection, there'll be far less difficulty working out a treaty."

Omrand spoke up angrily. "That isn't so. We may not be under an official deadline, but the governing board on Occuch expects us to complete our work as quickly as possible. If we take too long, this mission will look bad on our records."

At once the situation was clear. It was as Ryne had suspected. Omrand was far less concerned about the success of the mission than he was about impressing the men in those fine new buildings back on Occuch. Herril and the other old-timers had been right: the rutupis were taking over the Sternverein. Now they had extended their reach to the stars. Self-important careerists who couldn't fire a pistol, couldn't even do their own work properly, would soon be running everything. Ryne had been given a glimpse of this on Dumabb-Paraxx, and at the Sunden hearing; he should have been prepared.

He was determined that this mission would not be sacrificed to the petty interests of Omrand and his kind, but he knew he would need time. For the present, he had the situation under control. He did not respond to Omrand at once, but let the others speak. He was still uncertain of Locrin's position.

"The Secondary is right. It's understood that the swift completion of a mission is always preferred," said Angusel.

"We must not lose sight of the nature of the Sternverein," Omrand pointed out. "We represent a trading league. Defensive considerations are a subordinate part of our mission. Important, but always second to the commercial interests of the organization."

Locrin spoke at last. "Exactly right, Secondary. While I applaud Commander Ryne's zeal and dedication, I must remind him that this is not a nemesis run and he is not in command. In view of his outstanding record, I've been reluctant to exert my authority, but since. . . ."

"Wrong, Primary," Ryne said. "I'm still in charge. I'll let you know when I'm ready to release the mission to you."

"What do you mean?" Locrin looked up, her eyes narrowed. Ryne was sure she suspected a mutiny.

"Check the tapes on Third Contact procedure," he said. "The security officer is in charge of the mission until he informs the Primary that their position is secure. I haven't so informed you."

"But this planet is absolutely safe! You've been off hunting with the planetaries!" Angusel objected.

"I've been investigating, Tertiary. I'm not satisfied about our security yet. There are questions I want answered. I had hoped some of you would give the answers at this conference, but all I've heard is complaining about how the Korbians answer every question with another question, and never give you any answers. Stop making excuses. You're experts. The Sternverein has placed its trust in you. Find the answers." Keeping an alert watch on the others, he turned to his aide. "Walgan, you had some questions. Let's hear them."

"On the shaugarr hunt, the Korbians wore camouflaged hunting outfits. These would be functional if the shaugarr hunts by sight, but it does not. It hunts by smell. The outfits have no ritual significance. Therefore, we must learn precisely why the Korbians wear camouflage. It suggests the possibility of hostile intelligent life, and the Second Contact report says there is none on Mog Korb," the Under-lieutenant said briskly.

"Other settlements exist. We know that," Angusel replied.

"They are supposedly kindred communities, not hostiles, and the Dome People speak for all. Has the situation changed since the Second Contact team left? The Korbian pattern of travel suggests caution beyond a certain distance from the settlement. Are they wary of animals or humans? A conflict between settlements would complicate the mission," Walgan said.

"Of course it would. I certainly won't deny that," Angusel admitted irritably.

"Why didn't you find out? You're always with the Korbians," Locrin asked.

"They won't tell us. They simply say these are their hunting outfits and ignore any question we ask. They may be telling the truth, but I have to be sure," Ryne answered.

This seemed to trigger an outburst of curiosity on the part of the others. Other questions began to come forth. Ryne sat back, satisfied. He had bought time. The mission could still be completed successfully, to the mutual benefit of the Sternverein and the Korbians. That was his first obligation, and he was determined to meet it.

In a mere thirteen planetary days, he had come to like the people of the settlement. The others saw them as suspicious and evasive, mere obstacles to their own advancement, and condemned them without an attempt to understand. Ryne faced the unhappy fact that he had been assigned to a poor team. Angusel was weak. Locrin was interested only in succeeding on her first command, and Omrand was a careerist. They cared for no one and nothing but their own advancement. The Korbians were nothing to them. They wanted only to conclude a trade agreement and scurry back to Occuch to claim another meaningless award. Even the Sternverein seemed of little importance in their plan. If the agreement proved unworkable, they would remain safely behind their desks while blackjackets went off to fight. Men would die, and there would be much suffering. But the rutupis would prosper.

Tertiary Angusel looked up from her recorder. "Is that all? Are there any more points to be determined?" she asked.

"I have a question for you. What are *we* hiding?" Ryne asked. They looked at him and at one another in confusion, and he elaborated. "Milam believes I'm a hunter. Does he know what kind of hunting blackjackets do?"

Locrin looked about cautiously before speaking. "I'm not certain. I'll have to review the tapes of the earlier missions."

"When you do, find out what else we haven't told them. You're all calling the Korbians evasive and suspicious. Maybe the other missions gave them good cause."

"Which side are you on, Ryne?" Omrand asked.

"I'm here to benefit both sides. That's what a Third Contact mission is all about."

"The Korbians are a backward people. They don't know the true importance of their world and there is a chance that they might be obstinate, purely from ignorance," Locrin said. "I don't say that to condemn them, but to point out a possible problem."

"You've changed your views since planetfall," Ryne observed. "If you have any doubts about what side I'm on, speak up. That's an open invitation."

No one spoke. Ryne chose this as the proper time

to end the conference. He allowed six days for the others to gather their information, and set the next conference for the seventh day.

He spent the rest of that day with Milam's older children, who had greeted him at planetfall. The son, Geta, was friendly but not talkative. He seemed awed to silence by Ryne's mere presence, and anything Ryne said or did impressed him greatly. Ryne found his adulation awkward, but did not know how to prevent it.

Tereth, the daughter, was not awed. She had made herself Ryne's personal guide to Mog Korb and all things on it. As the trio traced the forest paths around the settlement, she picked leaves and fruits and explained their properties to him. Some of her explanations were beyond his understanding, but she was often helpful. He enjoyed his time with Geta and Tereth and found himself looking with reluctance on the team's dome when they returned. He would have preferred to stay with the family of Milam. But he had duties and could not choose for himself.

His guard turn was late that night. In the silence and the solitude, Ryne had time to think. He found himself troubled. Always before, on the driveships or on Occuch, there had been something to occupy his mind. Now there was nothing but memories of the past and uncertainty about the future. It seemed almost as if the Nolo effect were slowly wearing off. But that was impossible. He thought of all the good comrades dead on distant worlds, or aging slowly in planetbound stagnation. He remembered cold winds and hot sands, storms and battles and moments of pain and danger and triumph. He thought of Keela, and felt a longing that surprised and troubled him. But it passed in a moment, and his mind was at peace again. The Sternverein had been good to him, he knew, and he had given it his life in return. Now a creature like Omrand dared to question his loyalty.

But he could not condemn the Sternverein for one man, not even for all the false groundling heroes on

Occuch. They were talkers; they could not be judged by blackjacket standards. Still, it was for them, in part, that the blackjackets risked their lives. A sobering thought, that was, and a confusing one. Was he truly on *their* side?

When Walgan relieved him, he stayed for a time to talk with the younger man. Walgan had not been his choice for this mission, but he was doing well. He was young, but on his tunic he wore the emblem of the Combat Star.

"How long have you been a blackjacket, Walgan?" Ryne asked.

"I've lost track of the GSC time. About four years, bio-subjective, as close as I can figure, Sir. It gets confusing sometimes."

"It certainly does. You've seen some action, too."

"Yes, Sir."

"Nemesis runs?" Ryne said, hoping to draw him out.

Walgan nodded, but did not speak. Ryne persisted. "They must have been lively. You don't get the Combat Star for keeping your boots shined."

Walgan started to reply, checked himself, then blurted, "You do now, Sir. I didn't earn this the way troopers earned their decorations in the old days. I know I shouldn't say this to a Combat Commander, but it doesn't much matter any more. I'll do my duty on this mission, but as soon as we get back to Occuch I'm putting in for transfer."

Ryne was surprised by the outburst. He had not suspected Walgan of concealing such bitterness behind his silence. "You're doing a good job. Why talk of quitting?" he asked.

"You saw what it was like at the conference. That's what it's like everywhere in the Sternverein these days. Even the blackjackets are out for the decorations and the easy jobs." He pointed to the emblem of the Order of Leddendorf shining on Ryne's tunic. "I know what you did to win the Order. They tell all the trainees about it, and about what you did on

Hingwoll III and Maka Sicha. We leave Occuch with a lot of respect for men who wear combat decorations. But we learn fast," he said, his voice bitter. "On my last nemesis run, the mission commander and his two aides won the Order. Everyone else won the Combat Star."

"Must have been quite a battle," Ryne said.

"We shot six starved, terrified old men huddled in a cave. I got sick afterwards when I learned that their crime was violation of the Sternverein trading code. Men like you and Blesser and Gothrun and Kurtessus risked your lives against pirates and slave traders. Now they send blackjackets out to shoot down anyone who beats a Sternverein trader out of a profitable deal. That's all those six men did. And then they give us medals and tell us to wear them proudly."

Ryne was silent for a time. At last he said, "That's hard to believe, Walgan. I've been a trooper for a long time, and I can't believe that any of the men I knew would do that, even under orders."

"I don't think they would, either, Sir. But how long is it since you've been at the training schools?"

"Not since before I went to Dumabb-Paraxx. Maybe eight years."

"And a lot of that was at drivespeed. So it could be thirty or forty years GSC, couldn't it? And a lot of things change in that time. You might go back to Occuch and find the training schools full of spacetrash you wouldn't have allowed on the planet."

"I might," Ryne admitted. "But you came out of Occuch, and you're as good a trooper as I've seen. Now, listen to me. Once, when I was talking about leaving the Sternverein, an old. . . ."

"You?"

"Yes, me. I had some problems with people who didn't measure up to my standards of proper Sternverein conduct, and I was ready to dump my gear and hire out as driveship guard. No transfer for me, Walgan—I was going to desert. But I met an old trooper who talked me out of it, and I want to repeat what he said. He saw that the blackjackets' primary mission was close to completion; the whole organization was ready to move in a new direction. But the rutupis were trying to take over. . . ."

For the first time, Walgan smiled. He looked at Ryne and his smile broadened. "Rutupis! That's right, that's just what they are!"

"I agreed with him, too. And he said that if men like me quit, that would only make the rutupis stronger. If the Sternverein is going in a new direction, we ought to stay and make sure it's the right one. The blackjackets need you, Walgan."

"Do you really believe that, Sir?"

"I didn't desert, did I? Think about it."

When Ryne was alone in his private dome, he gave in to troubled thoughts. He could appear confident before a young trooper; alone, he wondered. If Walgan was correct, the Sternverein was going bad. He had suspected as much before this. Then, he had only worried about his own future and that of his comrades. Now he feared for Mog Korb.

CHAPTER 19

Ryne and Walgan spent more and more time among the Korbians in the days that followed. Ryne reasoned that close contact was necessary for the success of the mission. He had to know the Korbian ways of hunting and tracking, the land trails and seaways, if he was to gauge their defensive abilities. This was true, but it was not the whole truth. Though they could not bring themselves to state it openly, Ryne and Walgan had chosen the company of Milam and his people over the sullen presence of the other team members.

On the second day after the conference, the two blackjackets took part in a sea hunt. They went out beyond sight of land in the small swift Korbian fishing craft and spent the night on the gentle waters. When they returned to the settlement, they bore food for all. The sea creatures of Mog Korb were unlike any Ryne had seen before, but at the first taste he thought of the sotal fish of Jadjeel. Once again, this world had recalled to him his earliest home.

When they returned from the sea, a disturbing situation confronted Ryne. He found himself alone with Tereth. They were talking calmly about the events of the night. Without any warning he felt a sudden overwhelming awareness of her beauty and a great desire for her. It was as if a floodgate had opened deep in his mind, and the dammed-up emotions had surged up to take possession of him.

Terch sensed the change in him at once, and drew closer. "When you came to Mog Korb, I welcomed you as the woman welcomes her lover returned. Now I give you welcome as Tereth," she said.

He reached out to touch her face. "Tereth, I can't explain what's happening to me. This shouldn't. . . ."

"Do not speak of *should* and *should not*. It is my right to choose whom I will."

"But I have no right. . . . I can't accept. . . ."

"I choose you, Ryne," she said, embracing him.

Eagerly, he pulled her close. As she pressed tightly to him, a cold barrier shut in his mind. The Nolo in his system took control once more, and feelings bent to will. He released her and stepped back, shaken by what he had done, what he had desired to do. He might have wrecked the mission by one act of uncontrolled emotion. Something was happening to him, and he feared it would destroy them all.

Tereth looked at him, troubled and concerned. "What has happened, Ryne? You change so quickly. Come with me where we can be alone. The others know my feelings. No one will disturb us." She held out her hand to him.

"Tereth, I can't. Forgive me for what I did. I should never have touched you. I'll accept whatever punishment is due."

She was puzzled now, and he saw the hurt in her eyes. "Why do you speak of punishment? I have no wish to punish you. I have chosen you."

"What I did was wrong, Tereth. I'm under orders, and I must obey. Please understand."

She looked at him without speaking for a time, then said, "I will try, Ryne. But only because you are my chosen." Then she turned and left him.

He did not know what to do. He might already have ruined everything, and turned the Korbians against him and his comrades. Certainly, he had injured Tereth. But how could he explain what he himself did not understand? Such an outburst of uncontrolled feelings was impossible, and yet it had happened. Perhaps it was to happen again. He could only hope that Nolo would save him.

Ryne was certain he had violated some law of the Korbians, but nothing was said or done to indicate displeasure. There seemed to be no reaction at all. This puzzled him, but he kept a prudent silence, and decided to wait.

All became clear when he joined Milam and a large party on a trek to the farthest hunting grounds. This time they would face no shaugarr. They were after taftav, a small grass-eating beast of the inland plains. The taftav was the chief meat staple of the Korbian diet, and was hunted at regular intervals. This was to be the first hunt on these grounds for many transits.

They ended the first day's march early. Once they had made camp, Ryne was aware of a tension among the party, as if danger were at hand. He could discern no cause for it, but the signs were clear. Cooking fires were small and smokeless, and all were extinguished when the meal was done, well before dark. Men kept their weapons close at hand. There was little talk. Finally Ryne asked Milam about the danger. To his intense annoyance, the old man responded with another, totally unrelated, question.

"How has Tereth insulted you?"

"What? Tereth hasn't insulted me at all, Milam. What do you mean?"

The old man looked thoughtful. "Perhaps your ways are too different, but I had thought otherwise. Tereth has chosen you and given you signs of her choice. You have not responded."

Ryne hesitated. It was not easy to explain Nolo to an outsider. He felt himself on awkward ground. "I'm honored to know that she favors me, Milam. If I were able, I'd be happy to respond to her. But it's impossible. I'm on an important mission—as important for the Korbians as for the Sternverein—and I am not free to respond."

Milam seemed not to hear. "Tereth has not wished to choose before, and I was pleased to see her favor you. But you reject her."

"I have no choice in the matter. I can't. None of us can." Seeing the look of horror on his friend's face, Ryne quickly reassured him, "It's only temporary, Milam, for the duration of the mission. When we go on space duty, we're required to undergo a treatment that regulates our emotions and suppresses our sexual drives. This is Sternverein policy."

Ryne was not prepared for the old man's angry reaction. "A monstrous and unnatural policy! Why do you allow anyone to do such a thing to you? Are you all criminals, to be punished so?"

"We accept it freely, Milam. The alternatives are worse," Ryne said calmly.

"What could be worse than to become a thing that looks like a man but has no feelings?"

"You've never been in space. It's different out there. I don't know if I can even begin to explain it in words. It's so empty in those spaces between the stars. A man's emotions can tear him apart if he lets them—just the normal emotions of a normal man can destroy him, Milam. Imagine it—a driveship filled with men heading into mortal danger, thinking constantly of loved ones left behind. Wondering when they'll see them again, or if they ever will. And wondering, if they do return, whether their own children will recognize them. Time plays tricks on starfarers. The stars are hostile. A starfarer has to be totally disciplined, totally in control of himself at every moment, or he dies young."

Milam looked at him as if seeing someone new and fearsome. "You make yourselves less than men, less than women. You are not human!"

"We sacrifice something, for a time, in order to gain the discipline that keeps us alive. Our discipline has made us the greatest power in the galaxy, and we've used that power for the good of all human races," Ryne said.

"This is not discipline, Ryne," Milam said vehemently. "Discipline comes from within. It is freely chosen. You are slaves."

"Think what you will of us. No one forces us to undergo the treatment. We accept it willingly, in freedom, because we believe in our mission."

Milam was silent for a time, then he spoke in a

softer voice and his manner was gentle. "Forgive me,
Ryne. I was angry only because I have come to like
you. It is an awful story you tell. You allow others to
turn your humanity off and on as if you were no more
than a machine."

"It's for the good of humanity."

Milam sighed and shook his head. "Humanity survived long without the Sternverein, it will survive long
after the Sternverein is forgotten. The Sternverein
serves itself, Ryne, not humanity, and it uses you for
its own purposes."

"I can't agree. The treatment is not permanent.
When I complete my mission, I can be brought back
to normal in a short time."

Milam looked at him shrewdly. "Back to normal?
Then you know that you are not normal now—that
none of you are as you should be. And yet you say
this is right."

"Why didn't you ask the others who came before?
Surely you must have noticed," Ryne said. "Did you
question them like this?"

Milam made a gesture of dismissal. "We did not
care about the others. They asked questions to serve
their own purposes. You and Walgan ask many questions, it is true, but you partake of our lives and our
ways. We would have you stay among us."

"I'd like to stay here, Milam. Believe that."

"Then stay. Join Tereth and be a new son to me,"
the old man said.

"The only way for me to become normal again is
to return to my base for treatment. If I stayed here as
I am, I would only make Tereth unhappy. That must
be obvious."

Milam gripped his arm firmly, reassuringly. "We
can help you, Ryne. We have secrets the others never
learned."

"I thought our other teams learned everything
about Mog Korb," Ryne said warily.

"Some things were held back. We did not trust
them, Ryne. But we trust you."

"I'm grateful for that, Milam. But it doesn't solve the problem. I'm responsible for the safety of my ship on our return voyage, and when we touch down I have to deliver a full report on this planet."

"Why? Does your organization plan to attack us?"

Ryne was taken aback. "Certainly not," he said. "We want to help you defend yourselves."

"You have seen our world, Ryne. You have seen more of it than any otherworlder before you. Do we need defenses greater than those we have?" Milam asked.

"Yes, you do. You're not a warlike people. Your weapons are simple. Three fully armed Sternverein Security brigades could overrun this entire planet."

Milam shook his head sadly. "How little we truly know of one another, Ryne," he said.

Ryne leaned forward. He felt that he was losing something precious, and wanted to keep his grip on it. "Listen to me, Milam, please. I don't know how you feel about the Sternverein, or the others on this mission, or those who came before, but you've said you like Walgan and me. Trust us, then. We've dedicated ourselves to bringing law to the stars. I've known scores of men and women who sacrificed their lives to protect planets like Mog Korb from those who'd plunder and enslave them. It was done to my homeworld—that's why I became a Security trooper. I may lose my life in this cause one day, and I'll do it without regret. It's worthwhile. I'll sacrifice normal emotions, normal drives for a time, if I must. I don't believe it makes me a freak, or a monster, but even if it does, I'll still do it, because that's the price that I have to pay for the things I believe in."

Milam listened attentively, and thought over Ryne's words before replying. At last he said, "I know you speak the truth, Ryne. But you are a better man than the others. You are honest. The Sternverein is not."

"I hope to convince you otherwise."

"Perhaps one of us will change the mind of the other soon, Ryne," Milam said cryptically.

No more was said that night. At dawn, when Ryne awoke, he heard a stir outside his shelter. Milam entered as he sat up. The old man's manner was grave.

"Come quickly, Ryne," he said.

Ryne threw his tunic over his shoulders and stepped outside the shelter. The Korbians looked at him, but no one spoke. In the early mist, figures were ghostly and hard to distinguish. He looked for Milam and saw him standing by a tree. At his feet was a dark object. Ryne stared for a moment, then, recognizing the shape of a man, he cried, "Walgan!" and rushed to his side.

On the ground at Milam's feet lay the body of a Sternverein Security trooper. But Ryne had never seen the man before.

"He was spying on us in the night. Geta saw him and pursued. He raised his pistol, and Geta feared for his life. He threw his javelin without thinking, Ryne," Milam said.

"If he hadn't, Geta would be dead now. But I don't know who this man is or how he got here," Ryne said. He looked at Milam unflinchingly and added, "That must be hard to believe, but it's the truth."

Milam placed his hand on Ryne's shoulder and looked him in the face, gravely. "I believe you. But more than ever, I now believe that your organization is evil."

"There has to be an explanation. He . . . he may have been left behind by the Second Contact team," Ryne said. But even before Milam could speak, he knew this was not so. The man at his feet was no ragged starving castaway. The Sternverein did not leave men behind.

"We will find the explanation. Now, do as I say, Ryne. Geta will bring you a hunting outfit. Put it on. We have no wish to be seen," Milam ordered.

Ryne dressed quickly, his mind working furiously.

So these were, in fact, camouflage outfits. Then there was an enemy near. But what did that trooper have to do with it? His presence on Mog Korb was inexplicable. He could not conceivably have hidden himself on the *Kurtessus*. Had he come here before them, or arrived after? And what was his mission? If he had been trying to contact Ryne, why had he been so furtive? Every question Ryne thought of led to others, and there were no answers. But something seemed to be afoot among the Korbians. Perhaps the answers would soon be known.

They broke camp quickly and headed into the forest, where they followed a narrow trail. No one had passed this way for a long time. The trail was much overgrown, and their progress was slow. Silently, they moved in single file, about three meters apart. No one spoke. Ryne read the gestures exchanged by those ahead, and learned that the object of the hunt had changed. They were now after something more dangerous than a fat-haunched, slow-witted meat animal.

The signal came for a halt. Ryne looked down the trail for Walgan, and he saw him at last, far behind. He, too, was in Korbian hunting dress, not easily recognized at first. Ryne noticed that the men directly behind him carried javelins ready for hurling. When he reflected that Geta had downed a blackjacket before he could fire, Ryne began to wonder about the peaceful appearance of the Dome People. Perhaps it was all a deception. Perhaps Korbians and Sternverein alike had been lying to one another from first contact, and no one was to be trusted. If they did decide to use those javelins, Ryne thought, they would regret having left him his weapons. He would not die alone.

But even as he resolved to fight to the last, his resolution wavered. He could not hate these people. He could not bring himself to cut them down with the same unquestioning efficiency he had turned against so many starfaring evildoers and some who had done no evil at all. The Korbians were not criminals. They were defending their world, a task glorified by the Sternverein. Perhaps they were misguided; perhaps, in their fear and suspicion they had turned, unthinkingly, on one of their friends. That did not condemn them. They deserved the chance to explain themselves, and Ryne hoped they would be able to do so. He wanted them to be friends, not enemies.

Again, for an instant, he felt the stirring of emotion within him. It had never happened on a mission before; it was occurring disturbingly often on this one. He was more baffled than ever. He wondered, for a moment, if the food of Mog Korb had not poisoned his body, but rather, attacked his mind.

Milam appeared and gestured to Ryne. When they were apart from the others, Milam said, "We have crossed the blackjacket's trail. He came from beyond the cliffs. He was alone."

"Was he lost? A fugitive?" Ryne asked quickly.

"We believe he was a scout."

Ryne was startled. He did not accept this, could not imagine what had given Milam such an idea. When he said nothing, Milam continued, "Three will follow his trail. It will be very dangerous. Will you be one of them?"

"Do you trust me?"

"Yes."

"Then I'm glad to go along. I want to know about that blackjacket as badly as you do," Ryne said.

"Beyond the cliffs is the country of the Broadhand People."

"Are they enemies?" Ryne guessed.

"Not enemies, but not friends. Our people avoid each other, and there is peace. But when one trespasses on the land of the other, there may be battle," Milam explained.

"So if only three go, we may convince them that we're lost and mean no harm."

"No. If only three go, only three can die. Better three than the whole hunting party."

Ryne was impressed in spite of himself. He was rapidly revising his opinion of these people. "I understand, Milam," he said. "I'm ready."

Geta and a tracker named Plamar completed the party. As they prepared, Geta, without a word, handed Ryne the pistol he had taken from the blackjacket. He asked no return. Ryne thrust it into his belt, thankful for the gesture of trust.

The trail followed a deep ravine, then rose to parallel the foot of the cliffs. After some time, they came to a pass. Plamar led them farther on, to a second pass that was invisible from only a few meters away. It was the route she and her people used to enter the Broadhand territory.

At the top, they rejoined the blackjacket's trail. Ryne took two stims, for readiness. They were in open country now, and he felt unprotected even in the camouflage outfit. But he moved as the others did, staying low and moving with the breeze that stirred the tall grass into waves. Before long they reached the shelter of a forest. A short rest and they went on again, climbing steadily up a shallow gradient to the skyline. Geta and Ryne paused while Plamar went ahead. She returned moments later, her eyes wide. Her gestures were rapid, but Ryne followed them. He could not believe the message.

Plamar led them forward. At the crest, she pointed to a valley where the ground was level. There, on a landing ring, stood a white ship. Beyond it was a Sternverein Security trooper encampment, and beyond that, scattered at random in the clearing, were the shelters of Korbians.

Through his far-scan glasses, Ryne studied the scene in pained disbelief. Every sight proved deeper betrayal. The camp indicated a disciplinary team, augmented to forty-four men. A training ground had been cleared, and was even now in use. Blackjackets were instructing Korbians in the use of the pistol. Swinging the far-scan around, Ryne saw a guarded hut. As he watched, two blackjackets emerged carrying Rugatcz rifles.

Ryne lowered the glasses and stared blankly at the distant scene in sick bewilderment. This was a violation of all Sternverein principles. Planetary integrity was inviolable. Armament and training came only after a treaty, and after careful analysis of local hostility patterns and establishment of a monitoring procedure. The Sternverein did not speak friendly words to one people while arming and training their unfriendly neighbors. But the evidence of his own eyes —unless he was indeed going mad—suggested that the Sternverein were preparing a massacre of the Dome People.

He offered the far-scan to Geta, but the Korbian had no need of it. Ryne lowered his head, eyes tight shut. Even under Nolo he could feel the rage gathering as the full awareness of betrayal became clearer. The scent of betrayal befouled the soft breeze from the valley. The taste of betrayal was on his tongue, the feel of it on his fingertips. He felt a passionate hatred of everything he had once believed, everyone he had once trusted.

Absorbed though he was, the stims had sharpened his senses. He heard the telltale sound an instant before the others. It was an attack, and he reacted instinctively.

He rolled to one side and fired, downing the blackjacket before he could fire. A javelin crunched into the soil where he had been, and another hissed over his head. He fired twice more, and no more javelins came. Two of the Broadhands survived, and they took to headlong flight. Ryne rose to one knee, steadied his aim, and dropped both of them.

Plamar had taken a javelin cleanly through her side. Geta was untouched, and some of his earlier awe for Ryne had returned. Ryne directed him to keep watch on the encampment while he worked.

He dragged the dead blackjacket to them. Taking

up a javelin, he thrust it deep into the wound left by his shot. He put the blackjacket's pistol in his belt and placed his own in the hand of the corpse. That will give them a mystery to solve, he thought. They might be too busy to follow for some time. He turned at once to Plamar. Her wound was not serious, and he cleaned and dressed it quickly.

Geta turned and gestured anxiously. The shots had carried to the valley, and blackjackets and Korbians were on their way. With Ryne carrying Plamar, they started back to their own camp.

They arrived late into the night, exhausted, but Ryne met with Milam and the other leaders at once. He wanted them to know all he knew, and he wanted their counsel. He hoped, too, to hold their trust.

The Korbians listened attentively to him, and to Geta's and Plamar's supporting words. When all had finished speaking, they conferred among themselves while Ryne remained apart, dozing. Then Milam woke him and brought him to the group.

"We believed you, Ryne, but these events leave us puzzled. What would you do, and what would you have us do?" he asked.

Ryne shook his head to clear it, rubbing his eyes with the cold heels of his hands. He wanted a stim, but held off. He would need it even more in a short time. "I can't lay out a course of action yet. I want to go back to the settlement and find out all I can from the others on the mission." He noticed the glances exchanged between some of his listeners, and went on, "This must look suspicious to some of you. You fear that I only want to go back to bring word that the blackjackets have arrived. All I can do is assure you that I'm as surprised as you are. That second ship should not be on Mog Korb. I wasn't even aware of the second landing ring. The only explanation I can think of is that there's been some mistake."

"Your organization makes no mistakes, Ryne. They have told us this," Milam said.

"Then perhaps these blackjackets are renegades,

or even imposters, come to seize Mog Korb for themselves."

"Is this what you believe?"

Ryne looked around helplessly. "How can I believe anything now? With my own eyes I've seen impossible things happen. Things are happening to me—in my mind—that I can't explain. All I know is that the Sternverein sent me here with four others to try to persuade you that it's to your advantage to join us. We were not to threaten you, or use force in any way. That's why only five of us came, and of the five only two were combat trained—it's standard Third Contact procedure. We were to try to win you over by assistance and example. And now I've seen a white ship that has brought forty-four blackjackets here in secret, who are arming your enemies. This is a denial of everything the Sternverein stands for!"

Milam laid a hand gently on Ryne's forearm. "I think you face a crisis, my friend. You have believed in something all your life, and now for the first time you realize you have been deceived."

"The Sternverein. . . ?"

"They have spent much time among us, Ryne," Milam said. "Always, they questioned us about our world and our ways. They told us much about themselves in return, but we learned more from their questions to us than from their answers. They pretend to be what they are not. The Sternverein is a dangerous organization, capable of great evil."

"No, Milam. You don't understand at all. How could you? You haven't seen. . . ." Ryne paused, confused and fatigued, groping for words to tame the chaos in his mind. "Listen. The Sternverein was created to bring law to the stars. To protect helpless people, helpless planets. And it *does*. I saw it on my own homeworld, a world much like Mog Korb. A band of pirates overran my settlement. No one could stand against them. They killed my friends, my family . . . several times they nearly finished me. But the Sternverein sent one woman and one man, and they freed us. I helped them. When they left, they offered me the chance to go with them and become one of them. I've spent my life as a blackjacket, Milam. Suddenly to confront the possibility that I've been used. . . ."

"Perhaps the Sternverein wanted you because you had no one else. It could be everything to you—your family, friends, home, culture, even your religion. You would belong to it completely, and never question it," Milam said.

"But why would I ever want to question the Sternverein? Its goals were good, and it always worked for those goals."

"Always? Did you never doubt?" Milam asked gently.

Ryne thought of Sunden and the trial on Occuch. He remembered Hingwoll III, and Herril's words, and his talk with Walgan only a few nights ago. He did not have to reply. Milam read his answer in his expression.

"Go back to the others, Ryne. Find out what you must, and return to us. We will wait for you here," Milam said.

CHAPTER 20

Ryne rested briefly, then left for the settlement with Walgan. Geta and two other Korbians rode with them. Hard riding could bring them to the domes by morning of the day fixed for the second conference.

Weary though he was, Ryne could not relax. His mind was in turmoil. He had seen and done things he would have considered impossible. Far off, on a secret landing ring, a blackjacket force was defying the Sternverein code. He and the others had been spied upon by one blackjacket, attacked by another. And he himself had used his weapon against a comrade.

He thought long on Milam's words. The old man was wise and perceptive; Ryne valued his judgment. He had spoken of a crisis, and certainly a crisis was at hand. But the other things he said could not be true. The Sternverein could not betray its own ideals. It would not deceive a contact team. There had to be an explanation.

They arrived just after dawn. Ryne and Walgan went to their dome while Geta and the others went to inform the Dome People of developments. Time for the conference was close at hand. Ryne and Walgan were barely able to change into uniform, eat a quick meal, and down a stim. Locrin, Omrand, and Angusel had already gathered in the central dome.

"We didn't think you'd be back in time," Omrand said in greeting. "You've been gone for days, and sent no word."

"We're back. Let's begin," Ryne said brusquely, taking his place opposite them. Walgan sat beside him.

Locrin's voice was cold and formal. "As you say, Commander. I believe you had ordered us to provide certain information before you could see fit to relinquish command of this mission. There was a question of camouflage outfits. . . ."

"I've learned the answer to that myself," Ryne broke in. "The Dome People have planetary enemies. They're called the Broadhand People, and they live beyond the cliffs, far up the coast. I don't know why the other contact teams didn't mention them. In any case, they're now being armed and trained by a blackjacket force. I want to know why."

There was a moment of absolute silence, then Angusel, as if to verify his words, repeated, "A blackjacket force, you say?"

"Yes. There's a landing ring in Broadhand territory. They've built a base and training area around it."

"And where did you hear this tale?" Omrand inquired.

"I saw the base." Ryne thought it wise to hold back certain facts in his explanation. "A blackjacket spied on our hunting camp. We followed his trail and were attacked by another blackjacket and four Korbians. We got away, but not before we saw the entire installation."

No one spoke, and Ryne went on. "There are two possible explanations. Either there's been a disastrous failure of communications, or I've stumbled on a renegade ship. Those men may not even be blackjackets. They may have overpowered a troop somehow and taken their uniforms and equipment."

"Surely you can conceive of a third possibility," Locrin said.

"The only other possibility is that the Sternverein now violates its own principles, and I cannot accept that."

She looked to the others, then at Ryne, and said, "You may soon have to accept a number of things that are not to your taste. I can assure you that the blackjackets you saw are genuine and their mission is fully authorized. They arrived sooner than I had anticipated, but that's no matter. And since they're on Mog Korb, our security is no longer in doubt, so I am assuming full command of the mission."

"Who sent them here? We're a Third Contact mission. We have no need for a blackjacket force."

"Don't we? You yourself expressed concern for our safety at the last conference," Locrin pointed out.

"We're not made safer by distributing weapons to hostile planetaries. The Korbians we know are good people. Why arm their enemies?"

"There's been a change of policy, Ryne, and you have no choice but to go along. And you, too, Walgan," she said crisply.

The young trooper broke his silence. "I won't go along with a massacre."

"You took the oath, both of you," Locrin said angrily. "You're with us, like it or not, and you'll do the work of the Sternverein."

"The work of the Sternverein is to protect Korbians, not stir them up against one another," Ryne said. "We took an oath to bring law and justice to the stars. What's happening here is wrong. The Dome People are willing to be our friends, I know that. Even if they don't join the Sternverein right away, they'll remain our friends. Their enemies are our enemies. They won't turn on us."

Locrin looked at him like a disappointed parent struggling to keep her patience. She sighed and said almost fondly, "Ryne, you're dealing with something you don't understand, and you're talking foolishness. Do you really believe that the Sternverein has molded the greatest single force in the galaxy merely to protect savages and merchants? That might have been true once, but no more. You, and men like you—and we respect your courage, Ryne, whatever our differences—have risked your lives to make the stars safe and the inhabited worlds secure. And now we're moving into a new era, into something far more important, times more challenging than anything that's come before. Don't weaken now, Ryne. The real work is ahead." She leaned forward, her voice intense and urgent. "On Old Earth, before the time of Leddendorf, before even Wroblewski, there were some who dreamed of an empire that would span the stars. Then, it was only a dream; now it can be a reality. It will come, Ryne. It's still a long way off, and there's much to be done before it comes, but the empire will come. And when it does, a Leddendorf will rule it."

The news took Ryne unexpectedly. He looked to the faces of Omrand and Angusel. Both were alight with eager agreement for Locrin's message.

"It's true, Ryne. Sternverein technology is on a level with that of Old Earth. Most planetary systems are still relatively primitive," Angusel said.

"And you can't turn primitive rabble into citizens of an empire," Locrin added. "We have to do a lot of selecting. There must be discipline. The black-jackets will have important work to do in the empire."

He looked from one to the other, incredulous. "How can we even dream of such a thing? It would require millions of troops and better weapons than anything we've got. Even the weaponry of Old Earth would be inadequate to control a galactic empire."

"Our scientists know how to make fusion bombs and laser webs better than anything Old Earth knew," Omrand announced proudly.

"But they're incompatible with Wroblewski coils. What good is an armory on Occuch when the battle is on the other side of the galaxy?" Ryne asked desperately.

Locrin was triumphant. "The weapons will be where they're needed, Ryne. They'll be sent at sub-lightspeed to pre-set coordinates. Eventually there will be a bombship in orbit around every inhabitable planet in this galaxy. It will take a long time and a tremendous effort, but it can be done. And when it's done, no race will ever defy the power of the Stern-verein again. One hostile act and we'll obliterate their planet. The future is ours."

"Think of it, Ryne!" Omrand exclaimed. "For centuries, men have been forced to face the stars armed no better than a common soldier in the crudest days of Old Earth. Now we'll have weapons no one can withstand!"

"It's coming, Ryne. It's inevitable. The Dome People haven't earned the right to refuse us. If they try to hold us back, they must be swept aside," said Locrin.

"They won't refuse us!" Ryne said. They were confusing him with their talk of an empire, and selecting citizens, and a fleet of bombships. All those things were in the future, and might never come. There was a problem to be faced here, now, and it was urgent. He wanted to talk of that. "We have time. We can win them over just by showing them all the benefits we have to offer them. Why must we use force?"

Locrin and Omrand exchanged a glance. Locrin gave a curt nod of permission, and Omrand said to Ryne, "We don't have as much time as you think. Mog Korb is rich in the metals we need for a driveship industry. It's essential that we get the building program under way. The old ships are durable, but they won't last forever, and we'll need hundreds of new ones for the bombships."

Before Ryne could digest that bit of news, Locrin produced another, far more unsettling. "We have rivals. There's a planetary league centered on Mazat, and from all appearances, they're not friendly toward the Sternverein. They've begun to turn out new driveships. And since the loss of Dumabb-Paraxx, we consider it. . . ."

Ryne broke in, "The loss. . . . When? What happened?"

"We don't have full information. All we know is that there was an uprising of the Quespodons and the Sternverein has withdrawn from Dumabb-Paraxx. Temporarily, of course," Locrin quickly added. "No one drives the Sternverein off for long."

Angusel said, "So you see how urgent the situation is. The Sternverein needs Mog Korb, and needs it now. The wishes of the Korbians can no longer be considered. For their own benefit, we have to seize the planet. Within a generation they'll be thanking us for our decisiveness."

"Actually, Ryne, all this debate is pointless," Locrin said. "If we don't do it, the next team will. Why not get the credit?"

Ryne was as confused as ever. He could not follow their reasoning through to proper conclusions. Nothing they had told him was demonstrably false, but he felt that they were deceiving him.

"How many will die?" Walgan asked.

"No one need die. I think we can leave matters in the hands of the Security troopers," Omrand said. "After all, you people are trained for this kind of work, aren't you?"

"We're trained to execute," Ryne said.

"And to defend," Locrin quickly countered. Then, her voice more friendly than Ryne had ever heard it, she said, "Listen to me, both of you. I'm not supposed to reveal this, but I'm going to do so. One of the reasons you were assigned to this mission was to give you a chance to redeem yourselves." She pointed to Walgan. "You've been heard to criticize Sternverein leadership and policy, and your future with the organization looks bad. And you, Ryne. . . . You've gone even further! Remember that Sunden affair? You've been zealous in your performance of duty so far on this mission, but now you're coming close to insubordination. Do the job you have to do, both of you, and we'll all return to Occuch with a triumph on our record. It will make up for a lot."

The two troopers looked to one another. There was no need to speak. They had lived among the Korbians. Each knew his own convictions, and believed that the other shared them. And yet they had taken an oath. The Sternverein was to be obeyed.

Still, Ryne could not bring himself to say the word that would bring death to his friends. In the tense silence, Omrand stood, stretched, and said, "Take all the time you want to think it over, we're not in *that* much of a hurry."

"We could all use a mug of scoof to brace us," Locrin said, rising. "I'll bring some in."

Her footsteps moved behind Ryne and Walgan as she headed for her dome. Omrand talked on, but Ryne did not hear his words. He was wary, even here, among his comrades. This all felt wrong. Omrand and Angusel moving apart, Locrin behind them. . . . He drew his pistol and dropped from the chair, turning and shouting a warning to Walgan. Locrin's first shot tore a fist-sized hole in the back of his chair. She did not get a second chance. Her body was still rolling as Ryne dove under the table, firing upward, lifting Omrand off the floor with a slug right under the breastbone. Angusel turned her fire on him, but she was too slow. Ryne's first shot sent her crashing back against her chair and then to the floor.

Walgan rose unsteadily, clutching his side. He was pale, and the hand pressed to his tunic was bloody. Ryne helped him to the table and cut away the tunic.

"Is it bad?" Walgan asked in a strained voice.

"Getting shot is never good. You ought to know that much by now," Ryne replied, not looking up.

"What about the others?"

"Dead. A good thing you moved fast."

"You warned me, Ryne. Thanks."

Ryne grunted, his attention on the wound in Walgan's side. "I can't be sure, but it looks as though you were lucky. I'll get you into stasis fast."

"What for? We can never go back to Occuch. Not after this."

And he was right, of course. For the first time, the full consequences of his action were unmistakably clear to Ryne. Whatever he had once been, he was no more. He and the Sternverein had both changed, the Sternverein slowly, almost imperceptibly, he in an instant. The Sternverein had betrayed its founding mission; he had betrayed the Sternverein. The crisis

Milam had warned of had come sooner than he expected.

"We're traitors," Ryne said numbly.

"Depends on who's talking and who's listening. On Occuch we're traitors. On Mog Korb we may be heroes."

"Maybe. That means I'll have to patch you up myself."

"All right with me. You saved Milam."

Ryne examined the wound. Unenthusiastically, he said, "Shaugarr slashes are clean. This is messy. We don't have any choice, though."

"No choice at all," Walgan said weakly.

Ryne worked fast. He was a skilled mediciner, and Walgan's wound did not require any skill he could not provide. Once he had closed and sealed it, he left the young trooper sleeping soundly and went to seek out Geta.

The Korbians had heard the firing. They were curious, but would not violate the dome of their ship-kindred. Ryne explained the situation as well as he could. Some were dismayed, even horrified, at the thought of members of any bonding group turning on one another in violence. Geta, who had idolized Ryne from the start and never fully trusted the three negotiators, was more sympathetic. He did not approve of what had happened, but he conceded that Ryne had had little choice.

Tereth had listened silently to Ryne, and heard the remarks of all the others. When Geta had spoken, Tereth stepped to Ryne's side and announced, "The ways of our ship-kindred are sometimes hard for us to understand. But I believe that Ryne has done something very difficult and very courageous, and done it not for himself, but for us. We should trust him completely."

Her argument swayed the others.

RYNE took Tereth aside to thank her, and to try to explain himself. It was a task he found almost impossible—how was he to explain his lack of normal emotions when he could not even feel that lack? He knew that he had been happy with Keela and his other wives, and they with him. He knew that Tereth was a brave and intelligent woman, and very beautiful. She had chosen him. No one had ordered their match for the benefit of the Sternverein; it was her free choice. And he knew that once over the effects of Nolo, he would love her and be happy with her. But knowing and feeing are different universes. All the rational argument his mind could muster would not bring to life those emotions dulled by the Sternverein in the interests of discipline.

But he knew something was happening to him that he could not explain, something that promised happiness for Tereth and him. He had experienced emotions since landing on Mog Korb. These were spasmodic, unpredictable, little more than quick flashes of feelings, but they were unmistakable human emotions. The Nolo treatment was losing effect. Something here on Mog Korb was fighting it.

Ryne had hope, and a reason to believe that Nolo could be overcome. Milam had promised his help. The Korbians were skilled in the use of natural medicines, and somewhere on this world was a cure.

Ryne offered the gesture of reconciliation, and Tereth accepted it and returned it. "Tereth, if I've done anything to offend you, it was unintended," he said.

"I know that now. Our ways are different."

"But you once thought of choosing me, and I hope nothing I've done . . . I hope that the way I am. . . ." He touched her shoulders in a gesture of affection and looked down on her helplessly. This was beyond his power.

"I chose you, Ryne, and nothing changes that."

He did not know what more to say. That was good news, if he could indeed defeat the Nolo. If not, it meant bitter emptiness for Tereth. He could not hope to make her understand, but she seemed to sense his confusion and sympathize. In the Korbian language, especially between intimates, gestures were more significant than speech. Tereth said nothing. She touched his brow and lips, and after a last gentle caress, she left him.

He placed Walgan under the care of three elder Korbians, all of whom he had instructed in the use of Sternverein medical materials. He learned then that the Korbians had decided to place their full trust in him, and do as he asked.

It took only a short time to gather the supplies he needed. With Geta and sixty hunters, he returned to Milam's camp.

CHAPTER 21

The consumption of too many stims took their toll during the first day's ride. In the sudden onrush of fatigue, Ryne came close to falling from his mount before he recovered himself. Geta understood what had happened, and took charge. Even though several hours of light remained, he called a halt for the night.

Ryne let himself be led. Another dose of stim would bring a quick temporary recovery, but he could feel himself close to the danger limit. Already his fingertips were cold, his throat dry and painful. A muscle in his eyelid twitched wildly. He might have made it through two more stims, but that would be extremely risky. He needed rest for the work ahead.

He fell asleep at once and slept soundly until Geta roused him. The others were mounted and ready to move. Geta handed him a bowl of shing and a cluster of redfruits, and sat beside Ryne's pallet. Ryne ate without hesitation.

"Two riders have gone ahead. My father knows we're on our way," Geta said.

"Good. Thanks for stopping when you did. I probably would have taken another stim to keep going."

"The blue stones you swallow . . . ?"

"Not stones. A stimulant to give me extra energy when I need it."

Geta looked disapproving. "They leave you very weak. It would be best to use them no more."

"I won't. I only wish I could turn off the Nolo that easily."

"Nolo?"

"Another gift of the Sternverein. Much longer lasting," Ryne said.

It had never occurred to him before, but now it was obvious that the Sternverein had little trust in its troopers. They were given constant praise, but never freedom. Nolo kept them disciplined. Stims kept them alert. Marriage was made a reward for loyal service and a source of power for the organization. The individual counted for nothing. He was cut off from all outsiders, expected to associate only with other members, forbidden to question. The Sternverein, for all its proud boasts and imperial dreams, seemed to fear normal humans reacting in a normal way. Odd, how clear everything was now, when he had never been able to see it before. Perhaps much more would come clear to him in the days to come. He hoped so. There was much to be relearned.

THEY arrived at Milam's camp late in the day. Milam greeted them himself, and his news was not reassuring. The blackjackets and the Broadhands had already begun to break camp, and their scouts had started toward the cliffs. There could be little doubt that their destination was the settlement of the Dome People.

"This has never happened before, Ryne. Now and then, when someone violates hunting grounds, there is a battle. But never. . . ." Milam stopped, unable to find the word. His language had no term for *invasion*.

"No choice but to resist. And you'd be wise to make your stand here. We've got a good force."

"We have no weapons to match theirs," Milam said gloomily.

"You have a few now. I emptied out the weapons locker of the *Kurtessus*. Geta will distribute them."

"It takes time to learn to use new weapons well."

"I'm hoping we won't have to use them, Milam. I think this can be handled without weapons. I'm going to try. If this planet is to stay free, all Korbians will have to unite, and shedding one another's blood will only drive you apart. And I don't want to kill any more of my own people."

Summoning the other leaders, Ryne outlined his strategy. He was heartened by the news of the abandonment of Dumabb-Paraxx. It showed that blackjackets could be driven off. Of course, those were garrison troops, soft and unready for combat.

The invaders of Mog Korb were sure to be tougher than that. But perhaps Walgan had been correct when he spoke of the kind of men being turned into blackjackets these days. The specimens Ryne had seen on Mog Korb were not impressive. Perhaps, as their mission had become degraded, the blackjackets themselves had become less than they once had been. Ryne hoped this was so. If they were as strong and as dedicated as ever, there would be a terrible battle on Mog Korb this day.

As he readied himself, Ryne thought of his first home, Jadjeel, so like Mog Korb in many ways. Its people were merchants and traders, simple folk who shunned violence. He had joined the Sternverein to protect such people. He was one of *them*, not an empire builder for some faceless greedy entity called Leddendorf.

For most of his life, he had known only the Sternverein and its Security troops. It was not easy, even now, after all he had seen and experienced on this mission, to tear that part from his life. The Sternverein had given him strength and skill. He had lived a life of order, loyalty, and stern discipline, totally dedicated to a worthy goal. Never had he doubted those placed above him. Never had his comrades let him down. Always, in those vanished days, he had believed that if he lost his life on a mission he would be falling in a worthwhile cause, and his name would live on to inspire others. Now he was a traitor. All he had known was gone, an emptiness in its place.

Friends? None now but Walgan and the Dome People. Love? None that he could feel, though there had been love before, when it suited the Sternverein to allow it, and he hoped to know it again with Tereth. Achievements? Contributions to the galaxy? A small mound of corpses slain by his own hand. Future? At best, uncertain. Probably short. Whatever the Sternverein had given him, the price was high. He had paid in full, and owed them nothing.

THEIR force moved before dawn. With orders to capture Broadhands unharmed, scouts went ahead. The main body followed, moving fast. Ryne's plan was to confront the invaders as soon as they entered the territory of the Dome People, and he had a perfect spot in mind. Ahead of the pass in the cliffs, the ground sloped gently and passed between low hills to the ravine. Those hills would conceal his forces, while he met with their leaders on the open ground.

All went without incident. Ninety-three men, armed with javelins, concealed themselves in a loose circle among the hills. Fifteen more spread out behind them, ready to close off the pass at Ryne's command. Carrying a long-barreled pistol, Geta rode by Ryne's side. Ryne himself wore his baldric of decorations. It was instrumental in the plan he had in mind.

When all preparations were complete, Ryne and Geta rode to the open ground and waited. The others were under strict orders to remain hidden, and they obeyed scrupulously. Ryne searched with care, but could see no trace of them. Geta seemed apprehensive, so Ryne spoke to calm him.

"Will the Broadhands understand me?" he asked.

"Yes. We all speak the same language."

"Good. Are your people related?"

"Once, long ago, we were all one. The Broadhands were thieves, and the good people drove them out," Geta replied.

Ryne grunted and said no more. In his Cultural Groupings' work, he had come across scores of such stories, always used as an excuse for hating one's neighbors. At least the Korbians shared a language. That would simplify his work somewhat. But that work lay in the future. It was not yet time to think of it.

"They come," Geta said.

Korbians' eyes were far superior to Ryne's. He could see nothing. With the aid of the far-scan, he made out figures emerging from the pass. Some were on foot, and a few, in the lead, rode haxopods. At their head were two blackjackets and two Korbians, mounted, riding in pairs.

Ryne and Geta stood their ground, waiting. The Korbians saw them first. Through the far-scan, Ryne could see their excited gestures. When the black-jackets employed their own far-scans, Ryne gave the signal of recognition and summoned them forward. They talked briefly among themselves. The Broad-hands seemed reluctant, but finally the four leaders rode to meet Ryne and Geta. Ryne greeted them formally. They appeared totally bewildered at the sight of him.

"We weren't expecting to see you, Commander," one blackjacket said, speaking in the common star-faring tongue. "We thought the mission was in danger."

"Everything is under control now."

"What happened, Sir? We received a red-red emergency signal from the *Kurtessus,* but no message. I don't understand how you made it here." The black-jacket looked warily at Geta and the pistol he wore. "Are you in any danger?"

Ryne tried his move. It was a wild bluff, but if it worked, Mog Korb was saved. "I had to get here to prevent a planetary war. The mission was not in danger from the Korbians. Omrand was the danger."

The blackjackets were stunned. "The Mission Secondary?"

"Yes. Something—I don't know what—turned him homicidal. He killed two of us and wounded another before he killed himself. Someone must have signalled you, but I don't know who. I knew you'd assume an attack by planetaries, so I headed directly for the emergency ring to stop you," Ryne told them.

The blackjacket, an Under-lieutenant not much younger than Ryne, weighed this explanation. It did not seem to please him. Ryne, meanwhile, studied the gathering force beyond the four, and calculated the odds. Their numbers were not much greater, but they had overwhelming weapons' superiority.

"Omrand suddenly turned homicidal, you say?" the Over-lieutenant asked thoughtfully.

"Instantaneously. No warning at all." Ryne waited for them to take the bait.

"Just like Borgeri," the other blackjacket said. At this, the Under-lieutenant explained to Ryne, "The same thing seems to have happened to one of our troopers a few days ago. He was on patrol with some planetaries, and apparently he just started shooting them. He killed four."

"Has he recovered?" Ryne asked.

"One of the Korbians managed to get off a javelin before Borgeri shot him." The Under-lieutenant frowned. "For a time, it looked as though we'd have a war on our hands then and there. It was a job calming everyone down."

"I'm sure it was. Well, that's decided me, Under-lieutenant. This mission is terminated as of now. There are too many things the First and Second Contact teams didn't find out. I'll stay on and find out what I can, but clearly, this planet will not be ready for further contact for a long time," Ryne said. "Too bad you were brought down on a futile mission."

The others looked at one another uncertainly. The Under-lieutenant said, "Since we're on Mog Korb, Sir, it might be wise for us to check out your base. I'll have to report. . . ."

"Get off this planet as fast as you can. Blazing rings, man, can't you see that you're going to start a war if you violate territorial integrity like this?" Ryne said angrily.

"We were summoned on the emergency . . ." the blackjacket began, but Ryne cut off his argument.

"Now listen to me, Under-lieutenant. Your Korbians and my Korbians are enemies. I have to complete this mission and review the work of the earlier missions, with one injured man to assist me. That's work enough. I won't have you and your men stirring up a planetary war around me. Lift off, and lift off fast. That's an order. Understand?"

"What about mission security, Sir? If I report back. . . ."

"Security is my job, Under-lieutenant. Go back to Occuch and tell them Ryne is holding Mog Korb."

"Ryne?" The Over-lieutenant glanced at the baldric heavy with decorations. "I'm sorry, Commander. I should have recognized you at once."

"No offense taken. Just get going and let me get to work. I'll want you to leave me all the weapons you can spare."

The Under-lieutenant was taken by surprise. "For the planetaries, Sir?"

"Terms of the treaty, Under-lieutenant. If I decide to go through with it, I'll have to deliver. Have them here by midday, and lift off before dark." Ryne raised a hand to forestall the other's objection. "I can't allow any longer. The situation is too dangerous. If we delay, more of your men might go mad and we'll find ourselves in the middle of a war."

"Yes, Sir. As you order, Sir," the other said. He spoke to the Korbians in their own tongue, summarizing Ryne's order. When the Broadhand leaders started to dispute, Ryne broke in sharply, speaking their language.

"I am the leader of all ship-kindred, and I've ordered my ship-brothers to go to our homeworld and leave me here. I'm the friend and the defender of all Korbians. I will visit the Broadhand People soon, to prove my good will," Ryne said.

"You live in the camp of our enemies," the Broadhand said suspiciously.

Ryne gestured and said, "And my ship-brothers live in your camp. That does not make them enemies of the Dome People." Switching to starfarer's tongue, Ryne said to the blackjackets, "Get moving. You've caused enough trouble."

They gave one last salute, turned their mounts, and headed back toward the cliffs. The Broadhands were reluctant, but when their leaders spoke and pointed to Ryne, the rest followed. In a very short time, nothing remained but the dust of their passage. Ryne and Geta watched in silence until they had all disappeared even from Korbian view. Then Geta exclaimed, "You drove them off! All alone, you made them turn back, Ryne!"

"I just bluffed, and they believed me."

"But they are going," Geta said.

"They are. They'll be off Mog Korb by dark, and they'll leave weapons behind. Then our real work begins."

Ryne signalled for a scout, and passed the word that all were to remain in place until the blackjackets returned. He was well satisfied with the discipline of the Korbians. They had come here readily, willing to fight against heavy odds to defend their home. They were acting like trained troops. He had hopes for them, and for Mog Korb.

Just before midday, a party of blackjackets returned bearing a score of Rugatcz rifles, thirty long-barreled pistols, and a generous supply of ammunition. A young blackjacket was in charge of the detail. When Ryne had inspected the weapons and given his thumbprint in acceptance, he noticed the other staring at the baldric he still wore.

"Never seen decorations before?" he asked mildly.

"Never like this, Commander. You've won them all," the young man said in awe. "I never thought I'd meet you."

"Here I am."

"When I was in training, you were a legend. Everyone on Occuch knew about Ryne. You were the best."

"I'm still the best. Anybody who invades Mog Korb will find that out. You tell them that back on Occuch," Ryne said.

"No one will come to this system with you here, Commander. You're going to have a quiet stay," the blackjacket said confidently.

"I hope you're right. Back to your ship now, and good travel to you all."

The blackjackets rode off. When Geta assured him that they were gone, Ryne signalled for his forces to assemble and prepare for the return. He felt utterly drained, physically exhausted—but triumphant in a way he had never known before. He had won the most important battle of his life, and not a drop of blood was shed.

CHAPTER 22

Fires burned brightly in the forest camp that night. Ryne sat before his shelter, sipping shing and staring into the sinuous flames. The others were talking of the day's events, marvelling over the weapons and the way Ryne had made blackjackets and Broadhands alike do his bidding. He did not join in, but stayed alone by his shelter. It was a good time and place to think.

The blackjackets could not return in less than seven years GSC. If they returned after that, they came at their own risk. Mog Korb was not going to be enslaved to satisfy anyone's dream of empire. Perhaps one man could not stop the Sternverein, but he might slow it down. The Korbians had arms now, and they would learn to use them well. He would see to that. Now there were two worlds in resistance, Mog Korb and Dumabb-Paraxx. He had heard of others, and with the *Kurtessus,* he might find them. But much had to be done here before he could turn his efforts outward.

The thought of the bombships troubled him. Perhaps they were just another lie, a trick to win his compliance, but he could not be certain. He did not doubt that the Sternverein would use such weapons. Rutupis were not eager to risk their lives in combat; long-distance weapons were more their style. He pictured the future . . . the horrendous destructive power of Old Earth orbiting every inhabited world, awaiting the signal for annihilation. And when the Sternverein was long forgotten, the bombships might still be circling, waiting, murderous relics of a dead dream. It was awful to think on.

But perhaps without Mog Korb and its important rare metals, there would be no bombships. All the more reason, he thought, to keep this world free from Leddendorf's grip.

He wondered if there was any solution to the human drive for violence and domination. Long ago, on a world he could scarcely remember, he had learned of the Sternverein as a guardian and liberator. Now, a long lifetime later, he understood at last that we become the thing we destroy in the very act of destroying it. That is the great evil. There is no alternative and no escape.

He looked up to see Milam and Geta. The old man extended a fresh bowl of shing and they settled on either side of Ryne.

"You saved our world," Milam said.

"I got the blackjackets to leave without bloodshed. For that I'm grateful. But I can't save a planet, Milam. I'm only one man. I won't even be able to save myself when they send. . . ." He paused. Korbians had no word for *assassin* in their language. ". . . if they come back," he concluded. "But I can fight and teach others to fight after I'm gone. That's all I can do. I hope it will be enough."

"Today was a great day, yet you sound unhappy."

"I'm confused, that's all," Ryne said.

"Hear a story of our world, then," Milam said, and Ryne leaned back to listen. "You have seen the great hunting beast, the shaugarr. Every creature on Mog Korb gives way before it. The shaugarr's favorite prey is the taftav, a placid beast that feeds on leaves and plants. But sometimes, for reasons no one knows, a shaugarr becomes the protector of a certain herd of taftav. He will kill and eat those of other herds, but he defends his own. He guards them while they feed, watches while they sleep, and drives off all other shaugarr who come near. The taftav know this, and they trust him, even in birthing time."

The old man paused to sip his shing. Ryne said nothing, and Milam soon continued his story.

"A time comes when other shaugarr grow hungry for the flesh of this one herd, and no other will satisfy them. So they attack the guardian shaugarr and kill him. The taftav flee, but many are eaten. The survivors can only wait for another shaugarr to befriend them." Milam paused and looked searchingly at Ryne.

"Hardly a cheerful story, my friend. Am I supposed to be the shaugarr?" Ryne asked.

"That might be," Milam replied.

"But the Korbians are not a flock of taftav. You were ready to fight today."

Milam looked into the fire. "It is only a story," he said.

Geta looked up, and there was an expression in his eyes that Ryne knew all too well. "You can teach us to be shaugarr, Ryne," he said. "We will learn to defend ourselves without help."

Ryne nodded. It was as he had thought. There was no solution to the endless round of killing. If one existed, it was beyond his understanding.

He saw one sole hope. He turned to Milam. "When I told you of the chemical in my blood, you said you could make me normal again. I have some ideas about it, myself. Can we try to do it before I see Tereth again?"

Milam nodded. "We will gather what we need in the morning. Be confident, Ryne. We can find the way."

There was a chance. It was possible. Something in the food of this world, or the shing, or the flesh of the shaugarr. He would seek, and keep seeking, until he was human again, with human emotions. Perhaps in the experience of love, and concern, and sympathy, he would find the answer he sought; perhaps all the answers about this strange yet humane world.

Ryne had found a home at last. The days when his will was in the hands of others were now over. He had risked his life, stunted his feelings, sacrificed everything in order to bring law to the stars. But law was not enough. There was a higher goal, and from this day on he would pursue it. Now it was time to seek justice.

No more would he hide behind the cold barrier of Nolo and the armor of unquestioning obedience. There was another way, different from the way of the Sternverein and the shaugarr, a way beyond force and the taking of life. He would seek it. And he would find it.